"YOU WERE SHOT AT?"

Brian nodded enthusiastically.

"You're crazy." Alfie shook her head as she spoke, but Brian just grinned.

"Look, this doesn't make any sense. You think the man is a cold-blooded murderer?"

"I don't know. There's a lot we still don't know."

She stared at him, trying to read his eyes in the dark. She felt her heart race and wondered if it was out of fear or desire for him. Being this close was doing odd things to her insides. After a moment she whispered, "You should go."

"I can't just run away. I need to voice my suspicions. We might be able to expose him. If the man's a murderer—"

"No." She heard her voice tremble. "I mean . . . you should go. Leave my room."

He was still for a moment and she thought he might not have understood. Finally, he drew her closer. "I am not running from you, either."

Chasing Alfie

Sandra August

LEISURE BOOKS  NEW YORK CITY

In memory of my brother, Jack.

I need an answer, brother dear, that only you can tell,
Do they let you write in heaven, or should I ask to go to hell.

A LEISURE BOOK®

August 1999

Published by

Dorchester Publishing Co., Inc.
276 Fifth Avenue
New York, NY 10001

ISBN 0-8439-4566-4

Printed in the United States of America.

Chasing Affie

Chapter One

Denver, Colorado, 1872

L. V. Foster knew that it was unladylike to lift her skirts halfway to her knees and run. But it would be worse to miss the stage.

It was also unladylike to shout.

"Wait! Please wait!" she called with a gasp.

Well, that wasn't much of a shout. She was too breathless. She had been rushing around since she had first heard about the story, determined to catch this stage and not tomorrow's. She wanted to get the assignment over with as soon as possible.

A little mining town had experienced two murders, a common enough event and hardly worth sending a reporter. However, her boss at the *Denver Empire* had heard that the miners believed the murders had been committed by ghosts. Dead Indians, in fact.

Ridiculous, of course, and LV wasn't at all surprised that her boss would choose her—the only woman on the staff—to write the story. "You wanted more travel assignments," he had said smugly.

LV lifted her skirts higher and made another effort to shout. Next to nothing made it past her throat.

She watched the driver approach the coach and begin his climb to his seat. He was going to leave without her; she was going to arrive just in time to watch the coach rattle off down the brick street.

"Wait!" She would have waved her hands, but one held her carpetbag and the other her skirt.

The driver turned in her direction, probably catching sight of the wildly bobbing feather in her hat that threatened to come loose from its moorings, rather than actually hearing the pitiful croak that had come out when she had tried to yell.

After watching her for a moment with an enormous grin on his face, he dropped back to the ground and came to meet her. She was glad to know she was so entertaining. "You want the stage to Glitter Creek?" he asked.

She nodded, trying to catch her breath. He reached for her bag and she handed it over.

"Got a ticket?"

She shook her head.

The man chuckled. "You go get your ticket, little lady, while I tuck this in the stage for you. Is someone coming with the rest of your baggage?"

"No," she said, glad to have regained at least part of her voice. "There's only the one bag."

"Well, then, we'll be on our way as soon as you've taken care of that ticket."

LV smiled her thanks and tried to muster her dignity as she walked sedately to the office to purchase her ticket. In a few minutes, when she returned, the driver helped her into the coach. Her bag had been tucked under the seat, just inside the door—about two inches away from a pair of well-polished black boots.

The legs retracted, giving her room to enter. She took the seat across from the black-booted stranger. She had no other choice. The seat next to him was cluttered with books and papers, as was his lap. A rumpled-looking little girl occupied the other end of LV's seat.

LV glanced at the man, who had yet to look up from his work, then back at the girl. The girl watched her with suspicious blue eyes. Were they together? LV didn't think so. The man looked neat as a pin, but nobody had combed the child's hair in days.

The stage lurched forward, and LV's knees knocked against the man's. He deftly kept his papers from sliding off his lap and didn't spare her a glance.

LV eyed the open space between the girl's small knees and the seat full of papers. A trade seemed logical. It was, after all, four hours to Glitter Creek. They might as well all be comfortable.

Asking the man to rearrange all his books and papers as well as himself seemed too much to request, though. She leaned instead toward the little girl. "What's your name?" she asked.

The child turned away, mumbling something into the side of the coach.

"What, sweetheart? I couldn't hear you."

"She said she's not supposed to talk to strangers."

The man had spoken without so much as glancing at her. She should let his rudeness pass and concentrate on the child, but LV rarely did what she knew she should. "What about you?" she asked. "Do you talk to strangers?"

The head came up, and she found herself looking into intense brown eyes. He studied her as if she had asked a profound question. After a moment a smile lit his eyes but barely touched his lips. "The stranger the better," he said. "Brian Reed."

He held his papers in place with his left hand and stretched his right toward her.

"L. V. Foster," she said, slipping her hand into his. He raised an eyebrow, presumably at her use of initials, but made no comment. After giving her hand a firm shake, he let it go.

"The little girl was on the train when I got on in Kansas City. You weren't."

LV blinked. It was almost an accusation. "I live in Denver," she said.

He nodded, giving her stylish outfit a quick study.

LV had the oddest impression that she had been insulted but wasn't sure why she thought so. Other than being rather abrupt, he hadn't said anything inappropriate. There certainly wasn't anything suggestive in the way he looked at her.

With a start, she discovered that was the answer. She was used to being . . . well . . . admired. And this gentleman's eyes had already returned to his work.

LV frowned. In her interest in the stranger, she had forgotten about the girl. She gave herself one more second to scowl at Brian Reed's bowed head before she turned a pleasant smile upon the girl. The blue eyes were watching her intently.

"Nice Mr. Reed and I aren't strangers anymore," LV said. "I'm Miss Foster. If you tell me your name, we won't be strangers either."

The small blond brows pulled together. The little girl looked from LV to Reed and back again.

"I already tried that," Reed said, reaching for one of the books on the seat beside him.

LV pursed her lips and tapped a fingertip against them. She gave each of her companions a thoughtful perusal. One was willing to talk but wouldn't look at her. The other did nothing but stare.

Perhaps they didn't have to be friends for the girl to do what she suggested. "How about you and me trading places?" she suggested brightly. "You might give Mr. Reed more legroom."

The girl didn't respond.

"She kicked my papers," Reed said absently.

"So you scolded her and sent her cowering to the far corner," LV accused. This man's inability to take his eyes off his work bothered her more than it should.

But his head did come up. He cast the child a quick glance, then leveled his probing eyes on LV "I barely noticed."

Now, that she could believe.

His eyes remained on her for a few more seconds. Until he turned his attention back to the papers on his lap, LV couldn't pull her eyes away. She found the man most annoying. He could ignore her one moment and pierce her soul the next.

Maybe that was an exaggeration, but when he looked at her, all she saw were his eyes. Now, with his gaze elsewhere, she could remember his face. His long, straight nose was a little too big, his upper lip a tad too thin, his lower a bit too full. He was funny-looking, she decided, suddenly feeling better.

The coach had left the city and begun its climb into the mountains. She knew the road would get rougher and steeper as they went along. Her knees could well be bruised from knocking against Reed's if she didn't manage a switch. But if the girl was scared of Reed there wasn't much hope in that. She scooted farther into the seat, drawing in her knees as much as possible.

She turned to find the girl staring at her. These two were made for each other. She should ignore them both, but her curiosity was already getting the better of her. Why was the little girl traveling alone? How far had she come? There could be a great human-interest story here, certainly better than two murders being blamed on ghosts!

"Oh." Reed's head came up as if he had just been reminded of something important. "You might find her name on the paper that's pinned to her dress."

"Have you tried that as well?" she asked.

A ghost of a grin tugged at one corner of his mouth, his eyes laughing. He shook his head, then lowered it again.

LV took a slow, calming breath. If he thought it was funny that he irritated her, she would be sure to hide it in the future. With a smile firmly on her lips, she turned back to the little girl. "May I read that paper, please?"

The little girl nodded, turning in the seat to put the tag within reach. Simple, LV realized. People had had to read her tag all along her journey. LV cast a smirk over her shoulder, but of course Reed didn't notice.

The tag was crumpled, and LV smoothed it carefully. "Katherine Abbott," she read aloud. "Is that you?"

She watched the little girl smile shyly and nod before she looked back at the paper. "Deliver to Candace Dreher, Glitter Creek, Colorado. Who's Candace Dreher?"

Katherine stared up at her. LV stared back. Maybe she could stare her down.

Finally the little girl pushed her hair away from her face. "She's gonna be my new mommy," she said in a tiny voice.

LV's heart went out to the little child. "What happened to your old mommy?" she asked softly.

Katherine took a deep breath. "My first mommy died when I was little. Grandma Dreher became my mommy, but she died, too."

"No daddy?"

The little girl shook her head. "No daddies at all."

LV didn't want the little girl to dwell on her sadness. "I'm sure Aunt Candace will be thrilled to see you. Would you let me fix your hair so it'll be pretty when we get there?"

At Katherine's enthusiastic nod, she reached for her bag, trying not to bump the man across from her. At that moment the stage hit a rock, sending Reed's books onto the floor and Reed forward, almost into her lap. One arm, braced against the seat just above her shoulder, kept his weight off of her.

He was so close that she could see gold flecks in his eyes, smell some spicy combination of soap and musk. He didn't seem to be in any hurry to regain his seat. She found herself frozen, expectant. Of what? Of those lips that were mere inches away actually touching hers? Was she crazy?

Shock flickered in the man's brown eyes. She realized her breathing was labored. Could he guess what she was thinking? Still, neither of them moved until they heard the child whimper.

Reed jerked back into his seat. LV turned to find Katherine close to tears, her hands raised to avoid the papers that had landed around and on her.

"These won't hurt you, sweetheart," LV said, gathering them and passing them to Reed. Katherine tried to squirm out from under one last sheet. LV snatched it up, but the child still looked frightened.

"Didn't touch 'em, Mr. Weed. Honest," she said in a squeaky voice.

LV turned to Reed, ready to put him in his place if he so much as frowned at the child. But he had the most curious expression on his face. He eyed Katherine as if she were some puzzle to which he had nearly reasoned a solution. "Whose papers aren't you supposed to touch, Miss Abbott?"

The little girl bowed her head and answered contritely, "I shouldn't touch nobody's."

Reed looked mildly annoyed but kept it out of his voice. "Who told you this, Miss Abbott?"

"My turny."

LV turned to Reed to find his eyes on her as if he expected her to translate. She shrugged, more curious about how he planned to handle the situation than to whom the child referred.

Reed's eyebrows mimicked her shrug before he turned to the child. "Well, my papers aren't as important as your . . . turny's, whoever the hell—"

LV cleared her throat sharply, covering the word.

"—he is," Reed concluded, hardly missing a beat. He started shuffling through the papers, getting them back in order. As his attention was once again on his work, LV could feel Katherine relax.

With the crisis over, she looked down at what she still held in her hands. A newspaper clipping had been glued to a sheet of white paper. MINER SEES GHOST, read the headline. It was dated almost two years before. She skimmed the article, noting the location to be California.

The books were still on the floor where they had fallen, and she used the excuse of retrieving them as a chance to read the spines. One was on specters and the other on haunted houses. The third was on spiritualism as practiced by the North American aborigines.

Reed was reading up on ghosts. Research, she realized as she set the book and article on the seat beside him. He was after the same story, though he was taking the ghost part a bit more seriously than she was. She bit her lip to keep from laughing out loud.

A movement out of the corner of her eye reminded her that she had intended to brush the little girl's hair. With a smile, she grabbed up her bag and located her hairbrush. She slowly worked the tangles out of Katherine's baby-fine hair, which reminded her somewhat of the color her own had been before nature had decided to darken it to some unnameable color between blond and brown.

As she worked, she cast suspicious glances at Reed. He read his articles, referred to his books, and ignored her and Katherine. Let him write his story, she thought. With all this research he was bound to write some ponderous article that no one would want to wade through. This story wasn't worth the time. She would find the facts, write the item, and get back to Denver, where she would wait for the big story that would make her career. This, she was positive, wasn't it.

An hour into the stagecoach ride, Brian was glad for the research that kept his mind occupied. Every time he glanced out the coach window, his head spun. He either confronted vast, open space or a jagged rock wall so close to the coach that it could rip an arm off should one be so foolish as to poke it out the window. The current view was the former.

"Oh, look at the beautiful valley," the woman with the initials said. What were they again? LV? What could the *L* stand for that would be worse than being known as LV?

"Come here, sweetheart," she said, lifting the girl on her lap and holding her while she leaned out the window. "Do you see the pretty stream?"

Brian felt adrenaline tingle in his fingers and toes. He wanted to yank them both back inside the coach, but he knew it was irrational.

"There's a cow," the child said with a squeal. "I see a cow."

"A cow?" LV leaned farther out the window, and Brian tightened his grip on the book. "That's a deer," she said. "Don't you want to see it, Mr. Reed?"

He looked up to find her smiling sweetly. Had she already guessed his fear of heights? Or had she made it her mission to torment him the entire journey?

"Let me give you ladies more room," he said, stacking his books and sliding across the bench. At last, her knees would no longer brush against his. Maybe now he could concentrate.

When the telegram from Mr. Dale Wingate

had reached his office, there had been barely enough time for his secretary to put all the pertinent files in a briefcase as he'd rushed home to pack his bags. This sounded like an especially interesting case.

Wingate's telegram had said all his workers had walked out of his mine because Indian ghosts had killed two miners. Brian didn't believe the ghosts had killed the men. But then, he'd never had anything to do with Indian ghosts.

He suspected Wingate wanted him to come disprove the existence of the ghosts, which he was glad to do. Ninety percent of his cases turned out to be shams. He got paid either way. But it was the other ten percent that intrigued him, those few cases that defied logical explanation.

LV had settled into her seat, putting the girl Katherine across from her. He set his stack of books next to LV. She was trying to pretend she wasn't curious about what he was reading. He would have offered to let her read them, but he enjoyed watching her try to steal glances at their contents.

If his calculations were correct, they would be stopping soon to rest the mules. He looked forward to a few minutes on solid ground. Also, he looked forward to helping the young lady down from the coach. He hoped moving as he had to the other side wasn't going to interfere with that.

She was quite a lovely woman, all pink skin and golden hair. She was charming and friendly, at least to the little girl. He annoyed the hell out of her; that was obvious. He suspected it was because he was studying instead of giving her his undivided attention. Pretty girls were like that. But he wanted to go through all of these papers before he talked to Mr. Wingate. And, he noted, moving farther away from the young lady had not redirected his concentration.

But he couldn't help it. She was a puzzle that he couldn't resist contemplating. What was she planning to do in Glitter Creek? She had only one bag, so she obviously didn't plan to stay long. Had she found it necessary to leave in a rush? She'd be easy to follow; this stage went only to Glitter Creek and back. Besides, she had said that she lived in Denver, not that she was from Denver. She planned to return. Soon. Perhaps she was visiting someone for a couple of days.

He needed more information before he could reason her out. "Miss Foster, why are you going to Glitter Creek? If you don't mind my asking."

She looked a little startled. "Business," she said after a moment. "And you?"

"The same." He could hand her one of his cards. *Reed Investigations,* they read. *Specializing in Supernatural Phenomena.*

But that would satisfy her curiosity too quickly. He rather enjoyed her stolen glances.

Besides, after reading the card, she might not let him help her in and out of the coach. Some people seemed to find his profession a bit unnerving.

As expected, he heard the driver call to the team, and the coach slowed to a rocking stop. He opened his door before the dust settled and held a hand out to the lady. He was too late. She had already opened her own door and was climbing down unassisted. The child, Katherine, slid cautiously toward him.

He gave her an encouraging smile and lifted her through the door. Somehow it didn't seem right to set her down in the dust that still swirled around his legs. Balancing her easily on an arm, he carried her toward the dismal shack that served as the way station.

"We'll have some lunch here," the driver called as he unhitched the team.

"I'm sure it'll be charming," Brian muttered as he set the girl down near the front door. LV was waiting for them. She took the little girl's hand and led her inside. Brian followed. He heard LV ask for a place to wash up and wondered if the three of them weren't already cleaner than anything else in the house.

A large woman stepped away from a smoky stove and directed L. V. to a bucket of water in the corner. "The privy's 'round back, if nature's callin'," she said.

"Ladies first," Brian offered. LV didn't seem to take it as a gallant gesture. In fact, he thought he noticed a small frown before she smiled down at Katherine. The two of them went out a narrow door, and after a moment Brian followed, wanting to get away from the smell of burning grease.

He leaned against the doorjamb and watched LV and Katherine approach the outhouse as if it were some wild beast. Or perhaps they were expecting to find one inside. They eased the door open and peered around it. LV squared her shoulders and stepped inside.

Brian chuckled softly. This wasn't exactly what he was used to either. Glitter Creek, he hoped, would be more civilized. In less time than he expected, the two exited the outhouse and walked briskly toward him. Of course, the privy's atmosphere wouldn't invite anyone to linger. He stepped away from the door to let them back into the shack.

Katherine gave him a shy smile as she followed LV inside, but LV barely glanced at him. He didn't see how the outhouse was his fault, unless frontier manners required him to go first in the event of snakes.

He took his turn in the privy, then returned to the way station and washed up in the bucket the others had used. The smoke seemed more oppressive than ever. LV and the girl were standing close to the front door, viewing the cook with a certain amount of unease.

"Why don't we take our food outside and enjoy the mountain air?" he suggested.

"What a fine idea," LV said. "There's a robe under the seat in the coach that we can use as a blanket. Doesn't a picnic sound fun, Katherine?" In a second, both were out the door.

"Foolishness," the cook hollered after them. "Won't taste no different out there."

Brian didn't stay to argue. Outside, he found LV spreading a huge, hairy robe on the ground—buffalo, most likely. It looked only a little cleaner than the inside of the shack. But there were plenty of rocks around to sit on, and the outdoor air wasn't about to choke them.

Brian picked a spot near the robe and sat down. Katherine edged toward him. LV sat demurely on the edge of the robe and patted a place beside her for Katherine. The girl shook her head and edged closer to Brian.

"What's the matter, sweetheart?" LV asked.

"Is that a bear?" she asked.

Brian waited for LV to answer, but she seemed at a loss. Finally he came to her rescue. "Whatever it was," he said, lifting Katherine up to sit on his knee, "it's just his coat now."

LV gave him a perturbed glare. Well, what was wrong with that answer? He turned to the girl. "Do you want to eat up here with me, or sit on the bear's coat?"

"Buffalo," LV corrected. "I'm sure it's a buffalo robe."

"Can I 'tend it's a bear?" Katherine asked, gazing up at Brian.

He kept his face as straight as possible. "I am," he said.

"Then I'll sit down there," she said, grinning.

He helped her down and watched her sit, wiggling a little to get comfortable.

His attention turned back to the woman. "What does LV stand for, Miss Foster?" he asked.

"For the name my father gave me," she said, smiling sweetly.

He waited a moment. "You're not going to tell me, are you?"

"I've gone by my initials since I was a child. LV is my name."

"Really?" he said. "Here I had about decided you were a reporter, using your initials so your readers wouldn't know they were reading words written by a woman."

She stiffened. "Why should the readers care?"

Bull's-eye! "I'm sure they shouldn't, but occasionally they do. Or the editors think they do. Which paper?"

"The *Denver Empire.*"

He nodded, unfamiliar with the name but not eager to admit it. "Are you headed for Glitter Creek to report on the murders?"

She nodded, obviously irritated but trying not to show it. "And you?"

He hesitated. "I'll be investigating them," he said.

"Come and get it," the woman called. "I ain't cartin' this all the way out yonder."

Brian slid off the rock and offered a hand to LV. She came gracefully to her feet, which was a shame. He would have liked to have caught her if she stumbled. Katherine was waiting to take his hand, and together they returned to the shack.

The driver was seated at the table, digging into a plate of something. The woman stepped to the stove and filled three more plates, handing them off to Brian and LV. Brian, carrying Katherine's lunch, followed LV outside.

"Perhaps this wasn't such a great idea," LV said softly when they reached the robe.

"Why not?" Brian handed Katherine's plate to her along with one of the forks that he had stuck in his shirt pocket.

"Out here in the light, we'll be able to see what we're eating."

"What *are* we eating?" Brian asked, poking through the concoction with his fork. He recognized a carrot slice and maybe a piece of onion. "It's too thin for hash and too thick for stew."

"This," said LV, her eyes suddenly twinkling, "is grub."

"Appropriately named," Brian answered, straight-faced. "Bon appétit."

Katherine was the only one who seemed interested in food. LV, he noticed, picked over her plate, probably eating what she recognized. Brian ate only part of the meal as well. He could just imagine what the stage ride would be like with an upset stomach.

Soon enough they were climbing back into the coach. Brian was across from the little girl this time, LV next to her. He resumed his reading almost at once in hopes of missing any stomach-turning views from the stage window.

The two females put their heads together and talked softly. He tried to ignore them. The giggling, of course, was impossible to block out completely. After several minutes, he heard the distinct ruffle of a deck of cards.

He eavesdropped as LV explained the rules of some peculiar game. It wasn't poker; that much he knew. "Miss Foster," he said quietly, leaning toward her. "You realize you may be teaching that child something her aunt will consider sinful."

"We're not gambling," she said.

"That might not matter."

She leaned closer, practically hissing. "I don't see you trying to entertain her."

Her face was mere inches away from his, and she was scowling furiously. He glanced at the girl and found her watching them with concern. "I don't think we should fight in front of the child," he whispered.

Chapter Two

LV drew back, staring at Reed. Surely he was joking. Yes, she thought she caught a twinkle in his eyes before he hid them behind his books. But still, he might have a point. A point about the cards, not their fighting! She turned back to the little girl, smiling warmly. "Katherine," she began, "can you keep a secret?"

The little girl nodded.

"These cards will be our secret, then," she said.

"Ours and Mr. Weed's," Katherine added.

"Yes. We'll let Mr., uh . . . Weed in on our secret." She caught his brief glance and smirked at him.

LV patiently taught Katherine the basics of

cards. She was a quick learner and surprisingly competitive. Except for a brief nap after the next rest stop, the cards held Katherine's undivided attention. The girl, LV discovered, had just turned five and couldn't read, though she had begun to learn to count. It wasn't long before she could tell a club from a spade and had learned her numbers, at least up to ten.

As the stage rounded the last curve and approached Glitter Creek, Katherine stowed the cards in a favor of viewing her new home.

As they traveled, LV had been struck by the beauty of the mountains. Nothing, she decided now, could sully that beauty quite like a gold-mining camp. Tree-covered slopes had been denuded for lumber, and mines scarred what was left with piles of tailings. The town itself had grown with no plan, leaving the rutted streets to meander around the tents and buildings. The strike had come several years ago and had been profitable enough to encourage some more permanent construction, and she was happy to note the hotel sign on the front of a handsome three-story building when the stage stopped.

Reed sprang from the coach before it had finished rocking and held out a hand to help her down.

"What's going to happen," he asked softly as a hand on her waist steadied her unnecessarily, "when our girl tries to count beyond ten using jack, queen, and king?"

Before LV could think of a retort, he turned to lift Katherine out of the coach. He carried her the few steps to the wooden walk that ran in front of the hotel. She wouldn't worry about it, she decided as she turned her back to retrieve her bag. Katherine was now her new family's concern. And she certainly didn't care what Reed thought. She'd have her story in her editor's hand by evening tomorrow, while Reed would still be reading up on ghosts.

She nodded in formal farewell to Reed as she passed him. On the boardwalk, she stopped for a moment beside Katherine. "I enjoyed traveling with you," she said, extending a hand.

The girl took the hand gravely. "Will I see you again?"

LV crouched down in front of her, smiling reassuringly. "I'm only staying for a day, so I doubt it. But you're going to be so busy getting to know your new family, you won't even have time to think about me."

Katherine nodded as if LV's words were instructions.

LV couldn't resist giving her a quick kiss on the cheek before she hurried into the hotel. She had other things to think about, like getting her story. She stepped up to the desk. "I need a room for one night," she said.

Brian had been watching the exchange on the boardwalk when the driver, perched on top of the coach, caught his attention with a shouted, "Bag!"

Brian caught the luggage and set it with his briefcase, but by the time he turned back, LV had gone into the hotel, leaving the little girl alone.

"Who's going to deliver her to her aunt?" he asked the driver.

The driver dropped another bag before he answered. "I ain't got time. I gotta trade mules and get on back down to Denver. Ask the woman at the desk in the hotel. She gets paid by the stage line to sell tickets. 'Sides, I bring her enough customers that she owes me a favor." He tossed down another bag.

When the driver began to scramble off the coach, Brian eyed the two piles of bags. "Are all these yours?" he asked Katherine, pointing to the pile that didn't belong to him.

The girl shrugged.

"They're hers," the driver said, going to work on the team.

Brian left the bags on the boardwalk and stepped up to take the girl's hand. "Let's go see if the lady knows your Aunt Candace." Hand in hand, they went into the hotel.

The woman behind the desk greeted them with a smile. "I reckon a family man like yourself will be wanting a private room."

"Yes," Brian answered. "But the room's just for me. Katherine here's looking for her aunt."

He smiled down at her. "She's to be delivered to Candace Dreher."

The woman looked perplexed. "I know all the families in this town, and I never heard of any Drehers."

Behind them the stage driver chuckled, dropping Brian's bags on the floor. "You don't know all the women, Helen. Candy's one of Molly's girls."

Helen turned pale.

"Molly's girls?" Brian asked, then realization dawned. Helen wasn't likely to agree to deliver Katherine—not to that type of establishment. Still, blood was blood, and Katherine needed to find her aunt. "Could you point me in the right direction?" he asked the driver.

He chuckled again. "Cross the street, down the steps. That's San Francisco Street. Molly's house is to your right a mite. It's got pink trim."

Brian nodded. "I'll send someone back for Katherine's bags."

"You can't think to take that child to that house," Helen called after them.

Brian turned. "Do you have another suggestion?"

"Put her back on the stage and send her home."

Brian looked down at the bewildered little girl.

The stage driver spoke more gently. "I can't leave for an hour. You got that long to decide."

Brian carried Katherine across the rutted street. He already knew the girl had been sent to her aunt because her grandmother had died. Surely if there had been suitable relatives closer, she wouldn't have been put on a train somewhere east of Kansas City. It wasn't his place to second-guess what must have been somebody else's difficult decision.

He found the narrow stairs between two buildings and descended them slowly, mindful of Katherine's shorter legs. On the lower street, Brian stopped, feeling the effects of the altitude. "How are you doing, Miss Abbott?"

"Fine," she said, looking anything but.

A string of saloons, dance halls, and brothels lined both sides of the street. Most were quiet this early in the afternoon, but laughter and piano music issued from more than one saloon. Brian caught Katherine's hand and they started down the street in the direction they had been given.

Katherine said, "I hope Aunt Candace likes me."

"How could she not?"

"The big lady back there didn't like me."

Brian wondered if he should explain that her dislike hadn't been toward Katherine, but toward her aunt, or more precisely her aunt's profession. But then he'd have to explain just what that profession was. "Well, I like you fine," he said instead. "And Miss Foster likes you, doesn't she?"

Katherine beamed. "And we have a secret."

Brian nodded. "I don't think you need to worry too much about keeping that secret."

Molly's house was cream-colored, trimmed in a dark pink. A sign beside the door read, GENTLEMEN ONLY. Brian walked up the three steps and knocked.

A huge man filled the doorway. "We don't open till five," he said. He scowled down at Katherine, who shrank closer to Brian's leg.

"I need to talk to Candace Dreher," he said.

"Who is it, Rusty?" a woman asked from behind the giant.

"Some guy and a little girl to see Candy."

"A little girl?"

The man called Rusty stepped aside at the woman's nudge. Her eyes lit up. "My, my. You must be new in town. It's all right, Rusty," she said, dismissing him.

She drew Brian into the house and closed the door. She didn't seem to notice Katherine hanging on to him. Her elegant dress showed only slightly more flesh than was proper. Her dark hair was piled on her head in an elaborate fashion and adorned with strings of pearls. The smile on her lips was openly sensuous. "We don't officially open till five, like Rusty said, but I'm sure Molly wouldn't mind if we made an exception." She ran a painted fingernail down Brian's shirtfront, leaning close to his ear. "I'm Honey, and I'm much sweeter than Candy."

"I'm sure you are," Brian murmured, "but Candy's this girl's aunt."

"Let him breathe, Honey?"

Honey stepped away looking not at all guilty as another woman joined them.

"I'm Molly," the older woman said. "Did I hear right? This child is Candy's niece?"

Brian nodded. "So it seems."

Molly bent over, drawing Katherine out from behind Brian's leg. The woman's surprise was quickly hidden behind a smile. She straightened. "I'll tell Candy you're here. Come wait in the parlor."

"I'll show him, Molly," Honey said, taking Brian's free arm. "Can I get you a drink?"

"Get them both some lemonade," Molly said.

Honey escorted them into a tastefully appointed parlor that could have been in any wealthy home. He breathed a little easier when Honey left the room.

Lifting Katherine into one of the velvet-covered chairs, he crouched down in front of her. "How are we doing?" he asked, taking her tiny hands in his.

Katherine nodded. "Will I live here?"

"I don't know," he said. "But don't worry. I'll make sure you're safe."

Honey came back with two glasses of lemonade. Brian took them both from her and handed one to Katherine. Even the glass in his hand didn't keep Honey from rubbing up against him. "We could go to my room while the girl visits her aunt," she suggested. "First time's free," she said softly into his ear.

"You may have to dump the whole glass down her dress to cool her off," Molly said from the doorway. "Get back to your room, Honey."

Honey threw Molly a dark look before smiling back at Brian. "You know where to find me," she murmured and turned away. It was impossible not to watch her little behind as she slowly left the room.

Molly sighed. "I don't know what to do with that girl."

"No head for business?" Brian asked.

Molly smiled. "Something like that. What's this girl's story?"

"Orphaned."

Molly sighed. "Candy will be down in a moment. I hope you have another plan to fall back on."

Molly left Brian to ponder just what he should do. Katherine wasn't really his responsibility, yet he found himself in a position to make some very important decisions for her. He looked down at the little girl. "Don't worry, Katherine," he whispered.

She handed her half-finished glass of lemonade to him. "Are you worried?"

He set both glasses on a nearby table before he tried to answer. "Maybe a little," he said.

A blond woman came into the room, stopping just inside the doorway. Brian was struck immediately by her resemblance to Katherine.

His second thought was that the woman hadn't bothered to get dressed. A filmy dressing gown covered a few layers of similar material, and her blond hair had been hastily pinned up.

Her eyes flickered over Brian, then focused on Katherine. "This has to be Denise's child," she said, and burst out laughing. She had to grab the door frame to steady herself. "I need a drink," she said. "You want one?"

"No, thanks," Brian said, watching her move unsteadily toward the decanter and glasses that rested on the piano. "Clearly you are the child's relative."

She turned, amused. "I don't think there's any denying that, is there? See, Denise and I are twins." She sobered slightly. "Were. Am I to understand our dear mother finally kicked off, too?"

"So it seems." Brian edged closer to Katherine, resting a hand on her shoulder. "Katherine's traveled a long way to find a home."

"Home?" Candy laughed again. She tried to stop herself in the face of Brian's glare and walked toward him. "Don't you see how funny this is? I've been writing the old gal that I've got a store out here, you know, everything she wanted to hear. All so I'd get some of her hoard when death forced her to part with it. The last thing I expected to inherit was a child. Do you suppose the old shrew knew and this is her final trick on me?"

Brian didn't answer. He took a deep breath and wished he hadn't. Candy was standing too close and reeked of perfume and alcohol. "Miss Dreher, this is your chance to start over. You have a little girl to be responsible for. Why not try that store—"

Candy's harsh laughter cut him off. He let her wind down to an occasional chuckle between sips of whiskey. "Are there other relatives?"

Candy shook her head. "There are orphanages. Hey, why don't you keep her? Bring her back to me in about ten years."

Brian hastily lifted Katherine into his arms and left, Candy still laughing into her glass. He went out the front door, barely aware that Molly and Rusty watched him go.

They were back at the steps that lead up to Main Street before he set Katherine on her feet. He sat down on the bottom step and took the girl by the shoulders. "Is there anybody back home who would take you in?"

She shrugged. "My turny said he was glad to be rid of me."

There was this turny again. Brian frowned. "Well, I'm not. I'm glad I don't have to leave you. You can stay with me. I'll write some letters. We'll find out where you belong. And meanwhile, *I'll* look out for you."

He stood and started up the steps.

"Will you be my daddy?"

Brian stopped. She climbed up two more

steps and turned toward him. "You'll only be with me a little while," he said gently.

"My mommies weren't mommies very long, either."

Brian resumed the climb. "I don't know anything about being a daddy."

"Did you have a daddy?" she asked, catching his hand again.

"Well, yeah."

"What did he do?"

Brian had to think about that. "He went to work. He came home and read the paper." After more thought he added, "That's about it."

"You can do that."

They reached Main Street and stopped, waiting while a freight wagon passed. "Yeah, I guess I can do that."

"Good," she said. "I'll call you Daddy."

"Well," he muttered, "it beats the hell out of Mr. Weed."

LV stopped the rented buggy in front of the little shack. A sign above the door read, WINTER'S GATE MINE OFFICE. She had been told she would find Dale Wingate here. He had employed the two dead miners. She had intended to talk to the local law first but had found the office empty. She wondered if she had made it here ahead of Reed.

A tall, handsome young man came out of the office. He hurried to help her alight. "Jason Wingate, at your service, ma'am," he said.

"Please tell me there's something I can do for you."

She smiled. "I came to talk to Dale Wingate about the two dead men, but perhaps I can learn as much from you."

"Father's inside," he said, tucking her hand in the crook of his arm and leading her toward the door. "Surely you weren't sent here by that agency he hired."

LV frowned. "I'm a reporter," she said as he opened the door and then stepped inside.

"Reporter, you say?" An older, stouter version of Jason came around a cluttered desk. "Didn't know they let women be reporters."

LV gave him her most charming smile. "I can assure you that they do."

"Doesn't matter," he said, perching on the front of his desk. "Anybody who can get this damn thing settled and my men back to work gets my full cooperation. 'Less o' course you believe them fool ghost stories." He grabbed a half-smoked cigar out of a dish on his desk and thrust it between his teeth.

"I've never believed in ghosts before," LV said quickly.

"Good. Get her a chair, boy."

LV murmured her thanks to Jason and seated herself. "Now, Mr. Wingate, how long had you known the murdered men?"

LV questioned the Wingates for nearly half an hour, jotting a few things down on a small pad she kept in her reticule. There was nothing much that would help anyone solve the case, but there were some interesting details that would add to the story.

Jason walked her back to the buggy. "If you're alone in town, I'd be happy to buy you dinner," he offered.

"That's nice of you," she said, "but I have several more people to talk to this afternoon. There's no telling when I'll be free."

"Breakfast then?"

LV smiled. He was certainly charming, and she found herself tempted. But work had to come first. "I'll want to write the story early in the morning, if I've managed to talk to everyone. I'm sorry."

He helped her into the buggy. "I won't give up. The stage doesn't leave until three."

"Then I'll be seeing you, Mr. Wingate." She shook the reins and the horse moved forward lazily. She made a wide turn and waited as another buggy ascended the narrow road that led back to town. She recognized Reed's friendly face, and she smiled.

Instead of moving out of her way, he stopped his buggy beside hers. "Good to see you again, Miss Foster."

"Mr. Reed." She narrowed her eyes when she saw the girl sleeping beside him. "Why is Katherine still with you?"

"It's a long story," he said. "Could you take her with you? I need to talk to Mr. Wingate."

LV shook her head. "I'm going to see if the marshal will let me examine the bodies."

Reed made a face. "She can stay with me," he said.

"Good day, Mr. Reed," she said, feeling the press of time.

He nodded. "Ma'am."

In a moment his buggy moved on, freeing LV to maneuver down the hill.

Brian stopped the buggy and turned to look behind him. LV's buggy was already disappearing in a cloud of dust. Was she really going to examine the bodies? Surely not. She was probably joking. If she didn't want Katherine, she could simply have said so.

He turned back to the sleeping child. She had snuggled up so close beside him, he didn't expect to move without waking her, but he tried. He let her down gently onto the seat so he could climb out, but before his feet touched the ground, she awoke with a start.

"It's all right," he said quickly, seeing the alarm on her face.

Recognition dawned and she smiled. "You weren't going to leave me?"

"No," he said, smiling. "I was going to carry you into this building and let you sleep on my lap while I talked to Mr. Wingate."

Katherine scooted across the seat and climbed into his arms. He found himself suddenly glad that LV hadn't wanted to take her back to town. Somehow the feel of her trusting arms around his neck was a pleasure he wouldn't have wanted to miss.

The door of the shack opened before he could knock. "You another reporter?"

The question was asked by a man in his fifties, stocky and ill-tempered. A younger man stood silently behind him.

Brian shook his head. "Brian Reed, Reed Investigations."

"About time. Who the hell is this?"

"This is Katherine Abbott," Brian said. "My assistant."

"How do you do," Katherine said with childish seriousness. She extended a tiny hand toward the man.

Wingate almost took it. "Bah," he said, letting them inside. "I don't have time for foolishness. I need to get this mine back in operation before Glover hires all my men, and I have to train a whole new crop, if it ain't already too late."

"Yes, sir," he said, taking the seat across from the desk and adjusting Katherine on his lap. "Tell me who first presented the idea that your mine was haunted."

The sun had disappeared behind the mountain peaks when LV returned to the hotel. She requested a bath at the desk before going up the carpeted stairs to her room. The hotel was surprisingly elegant after the tents and shacks of some parts of town. But then she was paying for the elegance; or rather, the paper was. The hotel had no real competition and charged all the market could bear. She had noticed that the prices advertised by the business on Main Street reflected a similar philosophy.

She didn't have to wait long for her bath to be delivered, and as she soaked, she heard familiar voices in the hall. She didn't understand the words, but she was sure that the deeper voice belonged to Reed. The voices entered the room next door.

Or her imagination was playing tricks on her. Which, she decided, was entirely possible. Since she had seen the little girl next to Reed in the buggy, she had found her thoughts returning again and again to the child's situation. Had her aunt moved away? Died? Why was she still with Reed? It was a long story, he had said.

And likely an interesting one. Here was a child left in her grandmother's care after her parents died, then orphaned again. She was put on a train, then a stage, and now, evidently, had been unable to find her last remaining relative. This was a story to break a reader's heart.

And it was the anticipation of that good story that had her hurrying to dress. She certainly wasn't eager to meet her rival reporter. Though it would be fun to interview him for a story without his knowledge. She couldn't imagine a man thinking to write a story about the girl.

It was merely the luxury of the hotel that had her wishing for a better dress and taking extra care with her hair before she left the room. Or that was what she told herself. What Reed thought certainly didn't interest her. She stopped outside her neighbor's door and knocked before she remembered that she wasn't positive about the voices she had heard. She was preparing what she would say if complete strangers answered when the door edged open.

"It's you!" Katherine shouted, flinging the door wide.

"I was about to say the same thing," LV said, bending to hug the girl. "I thought that was your voice I heard earlier."

"Evening, Miss Foster." Reed stood across the room, adjusting his tie. There had been nothing wrong with the suit he had worn before, other than its being rather common. But in his new clothing he looked positively dapper, white shirt, black pants, black-on-black brocade vest, and the cravat he arranged so expertly.

"I was on my way to dinner," she said, wishing she could address the child but finding her eyes glued to the man. He was actually sort of handsome, certainly well built. The vest covered a completely flat stomach. "I wondered if you might like to join me."

"I'd love to," he said, lifting a jacket from the

back of a chair and coming toward her. "On one condition. Tell me what LV stands for."

"Good-bye," she said, turning to leave. She hated her name and hadn't revealed it to anyone in years. Leave it to this man to make an issue of it.

"Wait," called Katherine. "I don't care what Alfie stands for. Make her come back, Daddy."

LV stopped in her tracks. "Daddy?"

Reed stepped up behind Katherine and shrugged. "Alfie? You can call me Brian."

"Why would I want to know you that well?"

He laughed. "Come inside. If you'll fix Katherine's hair, I'll buy your dinner."

Katherine's eyes pleaded for her to agree. "It's a deal," she said, turning her full attention on the girl. Guiltily she realized that while she had noticed Reed's—Brian's—suit, she hadn't noticed that the girl had also changed clothes. "What a lovely dress," she said, walking with the girl to a small vanity, where an assortment of ribbons had been tossed.

"Daddy had the laundry press it," she said proudly.

"How clever of him," she said, giving him a glance. He was standing across the room, watching them with amused interest. He had donned the jacket, and it fit across disconcertingly broad shoulders that she hadn't actually noticed before. She turned away. "You pick out the ribbon while I take out the braid," she said.

As she brushed the fine blond hair, she glanced up to see the girl's reflection in the mirror. Brian had moved so that his reflection was there as well. She cast him a confident smile. Totally fake, but why should she care?

"I want this one," Katherine said. It was bright blue. The dress the girl wore was green.

LV considered a moment before she took the ribbon. The little girl's pleasure was more important than how she looked, she reasoned. She brought the hair together at the top of her head and tied it securely with the ribbon. Then she braided, turned, and pinned the slender lock to the back of her head.

"How's that?" she asked.

Katherine eyes turned to Brian's. "What do you think?"

He stepped forward. "I think I'll be escorting the two loveliest ladies in the territory."

Katherine beamed at LV and scooted off the chair. Brian took her hand and offered LV his elbow. She dropped it long enough to close the door behind them, and they walked leisurely down the hall. At the top of the stairs, Katherine giggled and raised her arms for Brian to lift her. He winked at LV before he lifted the girl and sat her on the brass handrail that topped the balustrade.

As LV followed slowly behind, Brian ran along beside Katherine, his hands on her waist as she slid down the rail. At the bottom, he set her on her feet and adjusted his jacket while she smoothed her dress; then they turned to wait serenely for LV.

LV wasn't sure how to respond. It was definitely not appropriate behavior, or wouldn't be accepted in the civilized world. It wasn't something she would have expected from the studious, preoccupied man she had met on the stage.

She decided her best response was no comment at all. At the bottom of the stairs, she took his arm again and let him escort her to the dining room.

"We need a table for three, plus one unabridged dictionary," Brian told the waiter.

The waiter, with a perfectly straight face, responded, "I'll see what I can do, sir."

LV didn't even try to guess. Perhaps he wanted the dictionary for use later in the evening.

After a few minutes the waiter reappeared carrying a small wooden crate about one foot square and three inches deep. "This way, please," he said, directing them to a table away from the few other patrons. "No dictionary was available, I'm afraid sir. Will this do?"

He placed the box upside down on a chair, and Brian lifted Katherine onto the top. "Perfect," Brian said. "Thank you."

The waiter held LV's chair, then left them to study the menus.

"I would never have thought of that," LV admitted to Brian.

Brian laughed. "I've had all afternoon to notice how the world's built for taller folks."

"Daddy thinks of everything," Katherine said.

LV smiled at her, then turned to Brian. "After we order, you'll have to tell me why she calls you Daddy."

"It's a long story," he said, turning his attention to the menu.

"I eat slowly."

He pinned her with deep brown eyes. "Tell you what. I'll tell you everything you want to know if you'll tell me what you found out when you . . . uh . . . examined the . . . " He made a face.

"Bodies?"

He nodded.

"I was asking about her simply because she's a mutual friend," she said, feeling the sting that always came with a little white lie. She reached for her glass of water, hoping it would shield her from those eyes that could surely read her thoughts. "Why should I give a rival reporter any information at all?"

"Because I'm not a reporter," he said blandly.

Katherine piped up. "He's with Weed Infestigations."

The glass had just reached LV's lips. She wasn't able to stop the laugh in time. She sat the glass down quickly, bringing the napkin to her lips, then dabbing at her dress. "Weed Infestations?" she suggested sweetly.

Brian gave her a pained look. From his pocket he pulled a small business card and handed it to her.

"Daddy's going to find the ghost," said Katherine.

Chapter Three

Before LV could ask for further clarification, the waiter returned for their order. She requested the same dinner Brian ordered for himself because her mind was too distracted to make a decision on something as mundane as food. As soon as the waiter left the table she leaned toward Brian. "You're going to *find* the ghost?"

Brian nodded, though with a touch of apparent self-consciousness. "That's what I do."

"What is what you do? You think those men were killed by ghosts? I can tell you right now they were killed by a tall, right-handed person with considerable strength."

He was keeping an admirably straight face,

but his eyes were laughing. It dawned on LV that she had just given him the information he'd been asking for. He *was* a reporter!

Interesting tactic, she thought. She had used aliases to get information on occasion, though it had never felt honest. Brian came equipped with business cards to lie for him. She sat back and glared at him, fighting the urge to grind her teeth.

"No, I don't think our killer is a ghost," he began, "but the miners have left their jobs because *they* think there's a ghost. Mr. Wingate hired me to investigate. I'll do my best to prove there isn't one."

Hmm, maybe he was telling the truth. What an incredibly odd occupation, LV thought, but at least he wasn't crazy. "So basically," she said, glancing again at the card, "you make your money off fools who believe in ghosts."

He winced. "You could put a better face on it than that, Alfie."

He was actually going to call her Alfie. Maybe she should call him Mr. Weed.

Before she could comment, he went on. "I relieve people's fears that their houses are haunted or that poor dead Uncle Ned can't manage to rest in peace. Usually, if I can find out why a ghostly presence was first suggested, I can determine what natural occurrences are feeding the myth."

"So in this case," LV asked, "what first suggested a ghost?"

"Well, according to Wingate, it's a legend almost as old as the mine. The ghost is usually identified as a woman. Several people have seen her. There have been a few odd incidents in the mine and in the office. Nothing serious, just things missing, objects moved around, that kind of thing."

"Which were probably done by other miners."

Brian nodded. "But once the ghost has been suggested, it's easier to blame it than to ask everyone who put a lunch pail up on the ledge."

"I see," LV said, not certain she did. "Why would they decide the ghost would take up murder?"

"Evidently, when the bodies were found, an old Indian was standing over them, saying the spirits of his people had taken their vengeance on the white man for despoiling their mountain."

"And this Indian was a ghost?"

"No," Brian said, laughing. "He's a harmless hermit who lives up in the hills somewhere."

"Maybe he's not so harmless."

Brian nodded. "I thought of that. Wingate dismissed the suggestion out of hand, but I plan to talk to the old man anyway."

They gazed at each other for a moment. Brian was probably mentally sifting through evidence, but LV was reassessing her opinion of him. Maybe he wasn't quite as odd as she had thought.

Or maybe his eyes were affecting her brain. She grabbed her waterglass for protection again.

"Miss Foster!"

Hearing her name called from across the dining room startled her into spilling a few drops on her dress. She brushed at them absently with her napkin as she watched the younger Wingate wend his way toward her.

"I see you found time for dinner after all," the handsome young man said. His attention turned to Brian only long enough to acknowledge his presence. "You can't imagine how disappointed I am that I didn't get here in time to share your company, but I can see you've already found someone to sit with. Unless he would care to move?"

"She's with me," Brian said quietly.

Jason frowned at him.

"And me, too," added Katherine.

Jason gave the girl the barest glance. "I hope to see you tomorrow then, Miss Foster," he said. He made a slight bow and moved away.

Brian watched him, his sharp eyes narrowed.

LV couldn't keep the smile off her lips. He wasn't as immune to her charms as she'd thought. He was jealous!

"The man knows more than he lets on," Brian said, and was immediately distracted by the waiter with their food. "Thanks. This looks so much better than lunch. Can I cut your meat for you, Katherine?"

LV stifled an irrational burst of irritation as she watched him slice the girl's beef into bite-size pieces. What did she care if he wasn't jealous after all.

"Where were we?" Brian asked, turning his attention back to LV. "Oh, yes. I'm going to look the Indian up tomorrow. Tonight I'm going to talk to as many locals as I can."

"How will you do that?" she asked.

"The next street down the hill," he said, tipping his fork handle in that direction, "is practically two solid blocks of saloons and the like."

"And the like," LV muttered. She glanced toward Katherine and was relieved to see she was intent on her dinner. "What do you plan to do with . . . K-A-T-H—"

"E-R-I-N-E," chimed in the girl. After finishing spelling her name, the little girl smiled proudly at LV and forked more food into her mouth.

"I'm impressed, sweetheart," she said before scowling at Brian.

"Well," Brian began, "I was hoping you . . . "

His voice trailed off as LV shook her head. "I have a story to write this evening."

"But you can do that in the morning. Your stage won't leave until the afternoon."

LV felt guilty already. She did her best writing early in the morning and probably would do little more than read through her notes tonight.

"Besides," Brian added, "she can be quiet and let you work. Can't you, Katie?"

At the little girl's nod, LV found herself nodding, too. She couldn't let him drag the little girl through such disreputable places.

"Thank you," Brian said, his relief obvious. "I promise to tell you everything I learn."

Hmm, she thought, maybe she would get something out of it.

LV scowled at the door for a full minute after Brian left. He was going to take Katherine next door, help her find a nightgown, then bring her back.

How had she gotten herself into this? It wasn't like her to get involved in other people's lives. Her own was enough for her to handle.

She was doing it for Katherine, she reminded herself, not the offbeat man who had talked her into it. The child had been through enough today; she didn't need to spend her first evening in Glitter Creek alone in a hotel room.

She still didn't know exactly what had happened to leave the girl in Brian's care. He had promised to tell her, but the subject had changed. Had that been deliberate on his part?

She shook her head to clear it. She was a reporter. She was an expert at getting information from people. She should have controlled the conversation and gotten the information she wanted.

Why hadn't she? Because his whole story about investigating ghosts had thrown her? Because he was more adept at directing their conversation than she? Because his intense eyes muddled her brain?

The knock on the door made her jump. She should have heard his door close and his footsteps in the hall. She took a moment to compose herself before she answered. A sorrowful Katherine stood there, clutching a bundle to her breast.

"Daddy's going to change his clothes and come say good night before he leaves. I'm supposed to sleep here if he's late."

LV wanted to grit her teeth. She smiled warmly at Katherine instead. "Won't that be fun! We can stay up late and tell stories." *Like why you call that crazy man Daddy.*

Katherine came slowly into the room and deposited her bundle on the bed, sighing softly.

"What's the matter, sweetheart?" LV asked, crouching in front of the child.

"What if he doesn't come back?"

"Well," LV said lightly, "I know he plans to come back."

"So did my first mommy."

LV nodded, sadly. A child this age shouldn't have such worries. "Things do happen," she admitted. "How about if I promise to make sure you find a home if Daddy doesn't come back?"

The girl smiled shyly. "Can I call you Mommy?"

LV laughed. "I think I'm more comfortable

with Alfie, all right? Let's get you out of this scratchy dress and into that gown before your daddy gets here."

Brian, dressed in clothes that would let him mingle with the miners, locked his door behind him. LV's door swung open before he could raise his hand to knock. He bent and scooped the little girl into his arms. "You be good for Alfie," he said.

Across the room, LV watched them. He couldn't tell what she was thinking. Perhaps she was unhappy at having the child to care for. It wasn't something he had planned on either.

"I'll try not to be too late," he told her.

"Oh, do stop by, however late it is."

Her voice was a little too sweet.

"I'm sure anything I learn can wait until breakfast. We wouldn't want to wake Katherine."

Katherine's tiny hand drew his face toward her. "I can wait up for you, Daddy."

"Better not, Katie," he said, lowering her to the floor.

"Alfie gave me some paper," she said, scampering toward the table that sat beneath the window. "I'm going to draw you a ghost."

LV moved toward him as the child moved away. "I'm sure Daddy will love that, sweetheart," she said.

Her eyes were on him as she spoke. He read

a challenge there and had a feeling he had missed something.

When she was close enough that he could smell the touch of perfume she wore, she said softly, "I think we can talk without waking Katherine. You still haven't told me about her aunt."

"I haven't?" He wasn't surprised it had slipped his mind. This woman was unusually distracting. And not simply because of her beauty. He had met many beautiful women who didn't befuddle him in the least.

She shook her head, causing a springy curl in front of her ear to caress her cheek. He imagined the curl wound around his finger, and he shoved his hands into his pockets. "Now what's it going to look like," he said just above a whisper, "if I come tapping on your door at two in the morning?"

She leaned toward him and his mouth went dry. He shouldn't be imagining himself kissing those expressive lips. They parted, and he tried to swallow. "Who cares?" she said softly. "I'm leaving tomorrow."

For a split second his confused brain wanted to believe he had heard an invitation. Then reason returned. He took a deep breath. It was a mistake. The scent of her made him want to kiss her more than ever. "I'll be here," he said, and he escaped into the hall.

He reached the top of the stairs before he

heard the click of the latch behind him. She had probably watched him walk away, aware, no doubt, of her effect on him. He didn't think much slipped past Alfie.

By the time he reached San Francisco Street, he had put the woman out of his mind. Almost, anyway. He looked up and down the crooked row of buildings, then decided that the Gold Rush Saloon was as good a place as any to start.

Inside, Brian peered through the smoke. The uneven floor and slightly sloping bar indicated the haste in which the place had been built. The sudden burst of laughter from the men at the bar illustrated how little anyone cared.

The bartender left the group, a broad smile still on his face, and he motioned to Brian. "Welcome, stranger. Always room at the bar for one more. What's your pleasure?"

"Got a cup of coffee?" he asked, stepping toward the bar.

"Just made a pot." He moved away for a moment and returned with a heavy crockery mug. "You new to the mountains?"

Brian nodded. He sniffed the coffee to gauge its strength, and decided it would eat through fine china.

"Good to steer clear of the spirits until you're used to the altitude," the bartender said. "You looking for work?"

Brian shook his head, setting the mug on the bar. If he inhaled too much more of it he was going to be awake all night. Drinking it was out of the question. "I'm looking for any of the men who used to work at the Winter's Gate Mine."

The bartender's friendly face hardened a little. "You the law?"

Silence fell around him.

"No," Brian said quickly. "I'm a private investigator."

Normal noise resumed almost instantly.

The bartender leaned one elbow on the table. "Glitter Creek's got a town marshal, but we elected him mainly to keep other law out. That works fine most of the time, but he ain't up to clearin' up no murder. Now poor old Wingate's mine's closed. Ain't nobody gonna work up there, what with the ghost and all. Not that anybody feels too sorry for Wingate. He hire you to investigate Perkins and James?" They were the two dead miners.

Brian nodded. "Can you tell me the name of anyone who has claimed to see the ghost?"

"Only a handful of people I know of. Two of 'em's dead. Couple more left for greener pastures. Floyd Trebly's seen it more than once."

Brian took a pad and pencil from his pocket and jotted down the name. "Perkins and James had mentioned seeing the ghost?"

"That's what I understand." He turned away, studying the group at the other end of the bar. "Hey, Thurston," he called. "You come talk to this fella." He turned back to Brian. "Thurston's always full of theories, but there might be something to 'em." He grabbed a bottle as he moved down the bar, refilling glasses as he went.

"What am I supposed to talk to you about?"

Thurston looked like every Easterner's idea of an old prospector. He had a grizzled gray beard, few teeth, and piercing gray eyes. He brought his drink with him.

"I'm trying to find out about the ghost that people say they've seen near Winter's Gate Mine," Brian said.

"Ah," he said, smiling. "I got it all figgered out." He downed his drink and set the glass on the bar. "But storytellin's thirsty work."

Brian turned to motion the bartender over and found him already on his way. "Want a little of this in that coffee?" he offered after refilling Thurston's glass.

Brian shook his head, imagining the noxious compound that would make. As the bartender moved away, Brian eyed his companion. The man took a tiny sip, smacked his lips, and started his tale.

"The way I got it figured, the ghost is old man Wingate's wife." He took a sip of his whiskey. "She died under mysterious circumstances, you know. Or that's what I heard." He took a longer sip.

Brian tried not to look surprised. "What kind of mysterious circumstances?"

Thurston shrugged. "Don't know. That's the

mystery." He drained his glass and looked at it significantly.

Brian turned to see the bartender headed his way. Once the glass was full, Thurston continued his story. "See, ol' Wingate was one of the first white men out here. He found the first gold, staked his claim, got some backing, and started his mine. By the time folks like me got here, he was pretty well established." He lifted the glass, drinking it halfway to the bottom.

"And?" Brian prompted.

"And he had a half-grown boy and no wife. Don't never talk about her." Thurston emptied the glass.

Brian didn't even look up. He knew the bartender was on his way. Thurston could probably keep the saloon in business all by himself. "She could have left him before he struck it rich," Brian suggested.

"This makes a dollar, friend," the bartender said, filling the glass. "I need to start collectin'."

Brian nodded and tossed a coin on the table.

Thurston shook his head, sipping the new whiskey as if it might taste different from the last, then took a huge swallow. "Nope. She's buried up there on the mountain. Don't nobody know what happened to her but Wingate and maybe his boy. Mysterious."

"What does this have to do with the murders?" Brian asked.

"I ain't quite got that figured out," Thurston

said, cocking his head to one side. "Do you suppose her ghost made them kill each other? Maybe old man Wingate killed 'em 'cause they was up there oglin' his dead wife's ghost."

Brian decided he had wasted a dollar. When the man's glass was empty, Brian slowly shook his head. Thurston didn't seem to be too disappointed. Or maybe he simply wasn't surprised.

"Do you know where I can find Floyd Trebly?" Brian asked.

Thurston shrugged. "He makes the rounds. Already been here, I think. You could try any of the other waterin' holes. He ain't welcome in the fancier places, though. He's a bit of a sot, you know? Hustles folks for drinks."

"Imagine that," Brian muttered. He took one sip of the coffee and wished he hadn't. "Have *you* ever seen this ghost?"

Thurston glanced at the empty glass. Brian kept his eyes fixed on the old-timer's face. After a moment Thurston shook his head. "Not me. Believe those who say they have, though."

Brian nodded. "Thanks," he said. With a wave to the watching bartender, he left. Outside, light spilled onto the rutted street from more than a dozen saloons and gambling halls. Mining the miners was evidently profitable.

Brian wished he could find Trebly without having to go into any more of the smoky establishments. But with no better idea of where to start except to skip the fancier places, Brian began his search. It was close to midnight when Floyd Trebly was pointed out to him.

Evidently Floyd had been drinking heavily since before dark. He was sitting at a table in the back corner of a little saloon, muttering to himself. Brian considered buying a bottle in exchange for information, but pouring more alcohol into the man didn't seem like a good idea. He slipped into the chair across from Floyd and waited for the man to notice him.

"I swear it's true," Floyd muttered. "Ain't never—" He hiccuped. "Course if I'us rich—" He reared back his head as if he intended to address the entire room and jumped to see Brian at his table. "Who are you?"

"Brian Reed," he said. "Can I buy you . . . something to eat?"

"Got supper right here," Floyd said, carefully pouring another drink with a less than steady hand.

"I'd like to ask you some questions," Brian said, "about the ghost."

"You come to make fun of an old man?" He peered at Brian with bloodshot eyes.

"No," Brian said. "I just want to know what you saw."

"Well," Floyd said, staring at the scarred tabletop, "I seen a ghost."

Brian gave him a moment to continue. When he didn't, he prompted, "Can you describe it?"

"It weren't no it. It was a she. That's for sure.

White dress flutterin' in a breeze that weren't there. Hair all streamin' behind her."

"Where were you?"

"Up the side a' the mountain. Not far from Winter's Gate. Right about where them miners was killed, actually."

That seemed like an odd coincidence. "Can you tell me exactly what you saw?"

"Glad to," he said after taking a drink. "She saved my life. That's exactly what happened."

Brian tried to keep his surprise from being too evident. "She saved your life?"

"It was like this," Floyd began, making two tries to get his elbow resting on the edge of the table. "I was goin' up the mountain to see Wingate. It was early, before dawn, but I knew he'd be in his office before the shift change." The edge in Floyd's voice indicated it hadn't been a friendly visit. Brian made a mental note to ask, but he'd let Floyd tell his story his own way first.

"Suddenly this odd breeze touches me, and I see this white figure glowin' in the moonlight." Floyd's voice became hushed. "I think it's the angel a' death come to take me, and there ain't no escape, but I turn to run anyway. I take about a dozen steps, and I feel the earth shake from the blastin' down below, and this rock comes rollin' down the mountain, takin' all its kin with it. Weren't exactly no avalanche, but I woulda got hit sure, if'n I hadn't run."

Brian remained silent, feeling goose bumps tingle on his arms.

"I looked back at the slide on the trail and there are some little rocks still bouncin' down and dust comin' up and all this stuff is just goin' right through the ghost. She's kinda hoverin' there watchin' me."

Floyd paused for a full minute, as if waiting for the image to fade. "I took it as a sign not to go see Wingate."

Brian let the man finish his drink and pour another before he asked, "Is that the only time you've seen her?"

Floyd shook his head. "About a week later, after I'd convinced myself all I saw was whiskey fumes, I went up there 'bout the same time a' day. I kinda hid, though, in case she was the angel a' death after all. Anyhow, here she comes, roamin' around like she's lookin' for somethin'. I stayed real still in case it was me."

Brian nodded. "And you've never been back?"

Floyd shook his head. "Go back all the time. Gotta prove to myself I ain't crazy. Course it just seems to prove to all a' them that I am."

Brian leaned forward, unable to contain the excitement that had been building as he listened to the man's story. "Can you take me there?"

Floyd took a moment to decide. "I'll draw you a map. You can go there yourself. I only seen her just before dawn, but maybe she's there all night."

Brian took a small notebook and pencil from his pocket and passed them to Floyd. "Would you meet me there?"

Floyd bent over the page, drawing hastily. "I'll see if I can make it." It took a moment for Brian to realize he meant it quite literally.

Floyd handed the notebook back and made a few comments on his sketch. Brian recognized the area as being on a footpath that would serve as a shortcut to the Winter's Gate. Part of the climb could be accomplished by buggy.

Brian was about to leave when he remembered his earlier question. "What were you going to see Wingate about?"

Floyd took a moment to answer. "I was goin' to talk to him about his boy, Jason. The son of a bitch cheated me at cards. But I decided the ghost didn't want me to bother 'em."

"But she saved your life."

Floyd nodded. "Yeah. But I think she was tellin' me she coulda taken it, too."

Brian digested this as he left the saloon. Outside, in the crisp, clear air, he felt his excitement return. He had to be on that mountain trail before dawn. And oddly enough, he wanted Alfie with him.

An insistent tapping on the door interrupted LV's vague, incoherent dreams. She tried to ignore the sound and cling to them but they were already fading. Quite suddenly she remembered Brian and his promise to wake her whatever time he returned, and she threw back the covers, grabbed her robe, and hurried to the door.

"Quit knocking," she whispered loudly. "You'll wake Katherine."

She flung open the door to admit a smoky-smelling Brian. "We're going to wake her anyway," he said softly.

"Whatever for?" LV asked, her exasperation showing. Being awakened too early had never been good for her disposition.

"To see a ghost."

LV stared at him as he closed the door and lit a lamp, turning the wick down low. "Why must Katherine see a ghost?" she asked, brushing an unruly strand of hair away from her face.

He had the nerve to laugh. "I want you to see the ghost, and we can't leave Katherine here alone."

LV yawned. "And why must I see this ghost?"

He pulled a watch from his pocket and tipped it toward the lamp. Evidently deciding he had some time, he rearranged the room's chairs and motioned her toward one of them. "I want you to be a witness."

She watched him sit but remained where she was. "And to think, for a while yesterday I decided you weren't crazy."

He laughed again. "I know how it sounds.

But there's a man who's seen this ghost several times. I think it's the ghost of Wingate's wife."

LV nodded. This was, of course, a dream. Brian was still tapping at the door. She just couldn't hear him because she was asleep. She knew this was true because if she were awake, she wouldn't be standing in her nightgown and robe, her hair tumbling over her shoulders, staring at a lunatic without feeling more upset than she did.

And there was nothing to do with a dream except play along. "When will we see this ghost? At the stroke of midnight?"

He seemed to find that amusing.

"I'm afraid it's too late for midnight. She's visible just before dawn."

"Here?" Even as she asked, she realized she wasn't asleep. Brian was really in her room talking about ghosts and she was really in her nightclothes. She tightened the robe across her breasts.

"Up on the mountain. We can go part of the way by buggy. I have one waiting outside."

LV shook her head. She wasn't going anywhere. "This fellow who told you about the ghost, how many drinks had he had?"

He hesitated, and LV felt a triumphant smile spread across her lips. "A couple, I suppose," he said finally.

She was surprised. "A couple of drinks and he claims he saw a ghost?"

Brian cringed. "A couple of bottles."

LV laughed and found it hard to stop. Fatigue, the absurdity of the conversation, and Brian's serious face contributed to her near hysteria. Fighting for control, she said, "It'll take two bottles for us to see it, too, I'd imagine. And since I don't drink, I'm going back to bed."

"What's so funny?" Katherine asked.

LV turned to find her sitting up, rubbing her eyes. "I'm sorry I woke you, sweetheart. Your daddy told me a funny story." She couldn't help looking at Brian to see his reaction. He looked only mildly perturbed.

"Daddy's going to go see a ghost," he said, rising and going to her bedside.

"Can I come?" The little girl threw off her covers and bounced excitedly.

"I want you to. We can have our adventure and come back for an early breakfast."

"We'll be really hungry," Katherine said, climbing onto his lap. "Can I wear the pants you bought me?"

"You bought her pants!" LV hadn't meant to say anything. She meant to let them leave and then go back to bed. What he did with Katherine wasn't her business. But the man obviously didn't have the first idea about little girls!

Katherine giggled. "He told the shopkeeper they were for my twin brother." She covered her mouth to stifle another giggle.

"My assistant has to be able to keep up with me while we investigate," he said, standing with her still in his arms. "Let's go get you ready." He turned to LV. "We'll see you in the morning, then," he said, and left.

LV looked after them, imagining the headline. INSANE MAN LEADS CHILD ON WILD-GHOST CHASE. ORPHAN GIRL DRAWN INTO LUNATIC'S BIZARRE BELIEFS.

What was she thinking? She threw off her robe as she rushed to her bag. Those two were a better story than the murders or the ghosts. And if she wanted to get the story, she had to go with them.

Chapter Four

LV held the lantern high with one hand and her skirts with the other as she made her way among the rocks that littered the slope.

"Hold up a second," Brian called from behind her.

She turned to watch him lift Katherine onto a boulder and sit down beside her, sighing deeply.

"It's hard to climb a mountain," Katherine said.

"You're doing great, Katie," he said.

LV was feeling the effects of the altitude, too, but evidently not as much as they were. Mainly what she was feeling was tired and grumpy. Coming up here to see nothing wasn't going to add but a sentence to any story. While she'd planned to question her subjects, the climb was too strenuous to allow for much talking.

"Why doesn't this thin air bother you, Alfie?" Brian asked, shading his eyes from the glare of the lantern she held.

"I left my corset at the hotel," she snapped, then wondered what had gotten into her. Women didn't mention corsets to men, even men as unusual as Brian Reed. Lack of sleep was affecting her judgment.

Brian stood and lifted Katherine. "Why didn't we think of that?" he asked, starting on as if they were on a picnic.

LV moved forward again, trying to provide light for his steps as well as her own. "How much farther?" she asked, hearing the whine in her own voice, yet not really caring.

"Katie," Brian said, still in obvious good humor in spite of having had no sleep at all, "as my assistant you need to remind me never to wake Alfie in the middle of the night."

Katherine giggled, and LV tried not to grind her teeth.

In a few minutes the slope leveled off onto a shelf. Brian set Katherine on her feet and fished a note out of his pocket. He stood close to LV as he studied it in the lantern light. The nearness of his body gave her very pleasant sensations, even with the slight smell of tobacco smoke that clung to his clothes. He emanated warmth and strength, and she caught herself leaning a little toward him.

I'm exhausted, she decided, drawing away. The lantern went with her, and he gave her a questioning look.

"This way," he said, taking the lantern.

LV caught Katherine's hand and followed Brian along the shelf. They made their way carefully around piles of debris from numerous test holes. She became conscious of how dangerous this could be, walking among these holes in the dark. Her hand tightened on Katherine's.

Brian stopped and turned back. *Wonderful,* she thought. *He's lost.* Then she caught the haunted look on his too-white face. *My God! The ghost!* "What is it?" she asked in a hiss.

He set the lantern on the ground and knelt in front of Katherine. "Can you stay right next to Alfie and not be scared, even if it's dark?"

She shook her head.

"What's wrong?" LV asked, squatting down beside them.

He came to his feet, keeping hold of the little girl's hand, and LV stood as well. "There's a body over there," he said softly.

"Who?"

He shook his head. "I need to take the lantern and find out. That'll leave you two in the dark for a few minutes."

"Don't leave me in the dark, Daddy," Katherine pleaded, clinging to his hand with both of hers and wrapping one denim-covered leg around his.

"I'll go," LV said, not particularly fond of standing in the dark either. Besides, she had examined bodies before and recalled clearly Brian's reaction to that fact. "You two stay close together and don't move."

She bent to get the lantern but Brian stopped her. "I don't like you going alone," he said softly.

His face was more in shadow than light, but she could read guilt there. He should feel guilty, she thought, leading them out here in the middle of the night. But something in her wanted to reassure him. She found herself saying, "Katherine needs you," before she turned away.

With the lantern in her hand, she started off in the direction Brian had taken. She heard Katherine whimpering and Brian comforting her.

Taking a deep breath, she reminded herself as she always did that the victim she was about to see could not hurt her. She had done nothing to hurt him. Someone else had. And that someone might have left a clue to his identity on the victim. She owed it to that victim as a fellow human being to do what she could to right this wrong.

It wasn't hard to find the body. Brian hadn't been that far ahead of them when he had turned back. It was a man, poorly dressed, lying facedown. If he was the drunk Brian had talked to, chances were that he had stumbled in the dark.

She knelt beside him, smelling smoke and alcohol, and felt for a pulse. The body was too cool to be alive.

"What did your . . . witness look like?" she called. She tugged on a shoulder, trying to turn him over.

"Forties. Hard up," came the answer. "Graying brown hair. Mole just under his left eye. Day's growth of beard."

"Very observant," she muttered, finally getting enough leverage to roll the body over. It was him, all right. The mole under his eye would have identified him even if nothing else did. And he was definitely dead. His eyes stared upward from a face frozen in terror.

"Talk to us, Alfie," Brian called.

"It's him," she said, holding the lantern to get a better look at the body. His trunk was soaked in blood.

"Did he fall?"

"If he landed on something sharp, maybe." With one hand she opened the bloody shirt. A gaping wound with straight edges answered his question. "No. It's a knife wound," she said, more to herself than to Brian.

"We need to go tell the marshal."

LV nodded. She paused to close the man's eyes, then rose to join the others. "Don't expect much from the marshal," she said as they started down toward the waiting buggy.

He eyed her quizzically, and she shrugged. "I talked to him yesterday and was unimpressed."

The walk was easier going down, and it wasn't long before Brian was lifting Katherine into the buggy while LV lit the headlamps. Brian helped her in beside Katherine. He then led the horse to a wide place in the road and turned him before climbing aboard and starting them back toward town.

"I'm sorry you didn't get to see a ghost," Brian said. LV assumed he was speaking to Katherine. She was glad that in the dark he couldn't see her roll her eyes.

"But I did see a ghost, Daddy," Katherine said. "Can we get breakfast now?"

"Did the ghost scare you?" LV asked, thinking of what her lantern must have looked like to the little girl.

"No," the little girl said. "She was pretty. Like my first mommy. She's a ghost, too, you know."

LV hoped Katherine's comments made Brian realize how his foolishness was confusing the child. Who knew what kind of nightmares this could all lead to? Exactly how to undo the damage was beyond LV. "As long as it didn't scare you," she said lamely. "We're all safe now."

There was enough pale light spilling over the eastern mountain peaks to make much of the town visible below them as they descended the twisting road. From this angle the haphazardness of the streets was more evident than ever. What odd collection of people would settle a community in this way? LV wondered.

Brian interrupted her thoughts. "Shall we eat breakfast first or talk to the marshal?" He sounded eager to do either.

"Breakfast," voted Katherine just as cheerfully.

"I think we need to tell the marshal," LV said. Both of her companions frowned at her. "All right. I'll tell the marshal while you two go back to your room and change Kevin here back into his twin sister."

Katherine giggled.

They had reached the edge of town, and Brian turned the buggy toward the hotel. "I think a twin sister should be your department, with the hair to fix and all." Brian flipped a loose braid as he spoke. "I'll find the marshal, then come back and take you ladies to breakfast."

When they stopped in front of the hotel, he pulled a key from his pocket as LV climbed out. He gave it to Katherine, who clutched it in her hand and let LV lift her down. "I won't be long," Brian said, and shook the reins.

LV watched him go, wondering if there was some hidden reason he wanted to see the marshal without her. She turned slowly toward the hotel entrance, Katherine's hand in hers. Perhaps this silly ghost-chaser stuff was all a ruse.

When he talked to the marshal, he would have to admit to being a reporter after all.

Or maybe it was worse than that. Maybe *he* had killed that poor man and brought her and the child up to see it to throw off suspicion. Maybe he was some kind of executioner for the mine. Maybe old man Wingate had brought him into break up any support of a miner's union. She'd heard of similar incidents. She hadn't even looked into that possibility.

She stopped outside her room with no memory of walking up the stairs. Katherine tugged on her hand. "My clothes are in there," she said, pointing.

"Sorry," LV mumbled. "I was just thinking."

She followed Katherine and let her unlock the door. Katherine skipped into the room, unconcerned about the chaos that greeted them. Clothes, suitcases, books, and papers were scattered everywhere.

"Daddy had all my dresses pressed," Katherine said proudly, pointing to the pile lying over the back of a chair.

"Which one will you wear?" LV asked, thinking of her own skirt, wrinkled from yesterday's travel. She had brought only undergarments and one fresh blouse.

"I don't care." Katherine pulled the top dress from the pile and headed behind a screen that hid a corner of the room. "Daddy says dresses don't matter as much as what you say and do."

"I agree," LV said. *And what exactly does Daddy do?*

While the girl was occupied changing her clothes, LV couldn't resist a little snooping. She could use the excuse of straightening up. The books, she noticed as she gathered them together, had no notes inside. The armoire was empty except for hangers, which she felt compelled to use for Katherine's dresses. The pages with the odd articles were evidently put away in the case, and she could think of no excuse to open it.

She was considering it anyway when Katherine came around the screen. She looked adorable in an Empire dress more appropriate for a little girl than the miniature adult dresses she had worn before. "Can you tie my bow?" she asked.

"Sure, sweetheart. Let me fix your hair." LV found ribbons amid the pile on the vanity that matched the tie at Katherine's waist.

"I want these," Katherine said, holding up a pair of dark blue ribbons that in no way coordinated with the pink and white dress.

"But these match," LV said gently.

"I don't want them to match," Katherine said, pulling the drooping ribbons off what was left of her braids and running a brush through the tangles. "Daddy says his favorite color is blue like my eyes."

"But," LV began, then reconsidered. The blue ribbons didn't look so bad with the dress, better than last night's choice anyway. And what difference did it make? Was she afraid the mismatched ribbons would reflect badly on her mothering skills? She had no mothering skills, nor was she interested in convincing anyone that she did.

"If that's Daddy's favorite color," she said, winking at the girl's reflection in the mirror, "we'd better wear something blue."

She brushed and braided Katherine's hair, berating herself for thinking that her own eyes were as blue as Katherine's, though somewhat darker. She didn't, definitely did not, care if Brian had noticed hers as well.

"Where are we eating breakfast?" Katherine asked as the door opened.

"On the other side of town," Brian said. "I still have the buggy, so you won't have to walk. My, but you look pretty when you're a girl."

Katherine giggled and flung herself into Brian's arms.

"You didn't spend much time with the marshal," LV observed, chiding herself for feeling left out.

"He wasn't in," Brian said, carrying Katherine into the hall and stopping to wait for LV. "I left a note on his door to find us at the Copper Kettle."

LV followed them to the stairs, then watched as Brian let Katherine slide down the banister again. The man was crazy, but he seemed any little girl's dream daddy. She stopped herself from even thinking what other dreams he might fulfill.

The rented buggy was just outside the door. It was nearly light out now, though the mountain still hid the sun. LV let Brian help her into the buggy and settled down beside Katherine as he untied the horse.

"Why are we going to the Copper Kettle instead of eating in the hotel?" LV asked as Brian climbed in beside them, rocking the buggy to Katherine's delight.

"The hotel dining room doesn't open for another hour, but that's not the only reason. The Copper Kettle's where the miners eat, though we may not hit the right time for a shift coming or going. Still, we're more likely to learn something there than at the hotel."

"We may learn about food poisoning," LV muttered.

Brian laughed. "I asked after the quality of food and the cleanliness of the kitchen last night."

"Asked of whom?"

Brian only laughed again. He directed the buggy down one twisting street and up another until he pulled to a stop on a steep hillside. LV gazed out at the building with a corroded washtub hanging by the door. It was built more into the mountain than upon it, and not carefully built at that. She was staring at the unpainted siding cut from at least four different types of wood when she discovered Brian standing beside the buggy, ready to assist her down.

She cursed herself as she took the offered hand. He'd think that she'd waited in the buggy just so he could help her. She was used to hopping out of the thing unaided and, double curses, he knew that. There did seem to be a touch of a grin on his face as she pulled her hand free, but with Brian, any number of thoughts could cause that.

She walked up the three steps without waiting for her companions and flung open the door. Tables and chairs crowded the uneven but well-scrubbed floor. The single room was lit by lanterns that hung on spikes driven into the solid rock ceiling. "A cave," she murmured in surprise.

"A mine," Brian corrected from behind her. He led Katherine around her and picked a table, settling the girl in without waiting for LV. He had manners enough not to take his own chair until she was seated. She took her time, enjoying the fact that she kept him waiting, then wondered what had gotten into her. She was here to get a story, not to flirt with someone. Especially not this someone.

Brian watched her with a hint of laughter in his eyes, as if he could read her mind. How conceited he would have to be to believe what she was almost thinking! After a moment she shook herself, wondering if his insanity was contagious.

A middle-aged waitress ambled up to their table. "Today's special is four eggs and a steak."

"Sounds good to me," Brian said. "Bring us three, if that's all right with the ladies."

"I want what Daddy's having," Katherine said.

"Make that two orders and an extra plate," LV instructed.

"Be right back with some coffee," the waitress said, "and some milk for your daughter."

Brian and Katherine were beaming at each other as the waitress walked away. Didn't either of them remember that this arrangement was temporary? She didn't want this story to have too heartbreaking an ending.

"You haven't told me why Katherine isn't living with her Aunt Candace," LV said, hoping to remind them.

Brian hesitated a moment. "She wasn't prepared to take the child."

"What do you mean, wasn't prepared? She is here in town? You talked to her?"

"She lives in a big, pretty house," Katherine volunteered, "with some other ladies and a man. One of the ladies really liked my daddy."

Brian looked slightly embarrassed.

"What do you mean, wasn't prepared?" LV repeated, leaning forward.

Brian leaned toward her, too, and answered softly, "Wasn't . . . sober."

LV raised her eyebrows. "The other women?"

Brian opened his mouth to answer, then closed it. His eyes seemed to suggest that she should figure it out herself. He gave his head the slightest tip toward the little girl.

LV drew back with an intake of breath. "A house of—"

Brian nodded.

"My God."

Before she could completely comprehend what she had just learned, a rumble started deep in the earth beneath them, grew louder, made the table tremble then shake. The lanterns above their heads swung, casting eerie shadows. LV clung to the table, expecting the ceiling to cave in at any moment.

The waitress, carrying a pot of coffee in one hand and two mugs in the other, strolled to their table and patiently waited until the shaking had subsided to set down the mugs.

"You shouldn't swear," Katherine whispered.

The waitress laughed as she poured the coffee. "That's just the miners blasting away down below. Happens twice a day, just at shift change. There'll be a passel of miners in here in a few minutes."

"I thought maybe it was the ghost," Brian said. LV blinked. He had said it with a completely straight face.

"Naw," the woman said. "She stays on her own mountain."

LV stared after her, then turned her quizzical

gaze on Brian. Without waiting for her to ask, he said, "The ghost of Wingate's dead wife. The mother of the young man who wanted to eat with you last night."

Several questions came to mind as she gazed at her companion, but she knew the answers to all of them. Yes, he did believe in the ghost. No, he didn't care if everyone else thought he was crazy. And, yes, he was, as a matter of fact, crazy.

She was considering saying as much when someone cast a shadow across the table. She looked up to find the town marshal, Hagman, glaring at Brian.

"You the fella left a note on my door?"

"Yes, sir," Brian said, seemingly unperturbed by the big man's manner.

"I don't appreciate being summoned like some lackey."

"I'm sorry if I gave that impression. Would you care to join us?"

He moved around to the empty side of the small table and turned the chair to straddle it. "Get to the point," he said.

"Certainly," Brian said. "We want to report a murder."

"Kill somebody, did you?" The man grinned.

LV rolled her eyes. She had listened to Hagman's idea of humor the day before.

Brian laughed as if he thought the man was funny, but LV could read the irritation in his deep brown eyes. "We found a body on the mountain along a footpath to the Winter's Gate mine. A man named Floyd Trebly. I had talked to him around midnight. We found his body shortly before dawn."

"We? Meaning you and who else?"

"Miss Foster and Miss Abbott."

Hagman turned to LV for the first time. "We met yesterday," she said with an insincere smile.

"Oh, yeah, the little lady who was so interested in the bodies. It ain't natural to be so fascinated by death. Especially for a woman."

Before she could retort, he dismissed her and turned his attention back to Brian. "If the body's where you say it is, Glover's crew'll bring it down. Ought to be comin' in anytime now."

"Marshal," LV said, "don't you want to examine the crime scene before the body is moved?"

"No," he said, giving her an annoyed glance. "Don't see why." He rose from the chair. "We don't need no outside law here," he said to Brian. "You Pinkerton or something?"

"Something like that. I was hired by Dale Wingate, but I'm hardly the law."

"Good," Hagman said with a cold smile. "I guess I won't have to run you out of town, then. At least not yet."

"Charming fellow, isn't he?" LV said, just before he went out the door. She fervently hoped he had heard.

She turned back to find Brian studying her, an unreadable expression in his eyes. Had it been anyone else, she might have thought he was attracted to her. But not this man; he was too fixated on his work. Still, why did that simple thought make her heart skip a beat? She couldn't pull her eyes away from his until his attention abruptly shifted.

The waitress set huge plates in front of them. LV consulted Katherine and moved part of her serving onto the empty plate.

"Yum," Brian said, winking at Katherine. "There's nothing like a good breakfast after a night of no sleep."

"You do this often?" LV asked. "Stay up all night chasing ghosts?"

"From time to time," he answered.

A growing commotion outside gave a half-minute warning before the restaurant was filled with miners. They looked tired and dirty but excited about the news of the body they had brought down to the marshal. It wasn't long before the room was filled with speculation that the Indian ghosts had struck again.

"That can't be right," said one miner.

Good, LV thought. *The voice of reason.*

"Old Trebly ain't worked for no mine for years," the fellow went on. "Them ghosts only want to stop the miners."

LV stifled a groan.

Another miner spoke up. " 'Less o' course them ghosts killed him for his firewater." A round of hearty merriment followed that suggestion.

Katherine seemed a little frightened by the noise, and LV tried to reassure her with a smile. As soon as they were finished eating, they made their way out of the restaurant. In the buggy, Katherine leaned her head against Brian's shoulder. She was nearly dozing by the time he stopped the buggy in front of the hotel.

Brian carried Katherine up the stairs and paused when LV stopped in front of her room. "I'm going to settle Katie in for a nap, then, after I take care of the buggy, try to get some sleep myself."

"Sounds like a good idea," LV said as she opened her door. "I have a story to write."

She meant to enter her room, but Brian had not moved away. She turned to find him watching her. There it was again. If she didn't know better . . . "Was there something else?"

He shook his head, but he seemed to hesitate. "Good luck with your story." Abruptly he turned away.

LV entered her room wondering about the awkward moment outside. Had he been waiting for her to volunteer to look after Katherine? She didn't think he would have hesitated to ask. It must have been something else. She had her writing materials out and was seated at the little table before it occurred to her that he might have wanted to say good-bye.

* * *

"Go to sleep, Katie," Brian said softly. "Alfie's right next door, and I won't be gone long."

He smoothed the fine blond hair away from her forehead and watched her close her eyes. She was such a sweet little thing, so innocent and trusting. His urge to protect her was frightening and gratifying at the same time. He waited until she was sleeping soundly before he quietly left the room.

A few minutes later, having returned the horse and buggy to the livery, he reentered the hotel. He paused outside Alfie's room, took a deep breath, and knocked.

"Come in," came the answer in a preoccupied tone.

He opened the door and stepped inside. She was sitting at the table, her head bent, the sun streaking her hair with shining gold. He was in town chasing ghosts, but he'd much rather be chasing Alfie.

He waited silently for her to glance up, looking forward to seeing her expressive eyes.

He didn't have to wait long. She evidently finished the sentence she had been writing. "I thought you were going to rest."

She didn't seem nearly as disappointed to see him as she might have. "I will," he said, pleased as always by her direct gaze. "I just wanted to ask you something."

"By all means, ask away."

He might have smiled at her resigned tone,

but he was a little too nervous. For the first time that he could remember, what someone thought of him really mattered. He was prepared to share something with her that he had never told another soul, not even his partners at his investigation company.

He took the empty chair that stood on the other side of the table and moved it closer to her before he sat down. He had already planned to begin with a question, draw her out a little before he offered his story. On the way here it had seemed like a good lead-in. Now it seemed like a stall.

She eyed him warily. "Is it that serious?"

"No." He forced a grin. "Why are you fascinated by death?"

She rolled her eyes and he plunged ahead. "I mean, I know why I am, but what's your story?"

She looked exasperated, and he realized he was interrupting her writing with something she saw as trivial. While he would rather see that beautiful face smile at him, watching her frown was better than going off to his room and never seeing her again. And she would leave as soon as she finished her story; he was sure of that.

"I'm not fascinated by death," she stated succinctly.

"But you're willing to examine dead bodies. Willing? Hell! You're almost eager."

"Eager for what I can learn," she explained.

She paused a moment, toyed with her pen, as if deciding what to tell him or where to begin. Or how to tell him to go to hell.

Finally, taking a deep breath that did interesting things to the fabric of her blouse, she turned her level gaze back on him. "I got the job at the paper on the strength of a story I sent them. The boss didn't know he had hired a woman until I reported for work the first day. He was furious. He tried to fire me not five minutes after I walked in the door."

Brian could imagine her reaction to that and wished he had been around to see it. "Tried?" he prompted.

"Well, I told him what I thought of the situation, and he backed down."

She was no longer meeting his gaze, and he knew there was more. "Just like that?"

She tapped the butt of her pen against her lips. "I may have mentioned that my father was Levi Foster. Mayor Foster at the time."

Brian grinned. "But what does that have to do with dead bodies, or do you imagine each one is your boss?"

She laughed and he got to see her smile. He was unusually pleased with himself.

"The boss decided that if he didn't dare fire me, he would encourage me to quit. He assigned me to all the murder cases. Which, by the way, was much better than sending me to all the soirees in town. *That* would have made me quit."

Brian smiled, thrilled that he already knew her better than her boss did. "Didn't it bother you?" he asked.

She shrugged. "At first, I suppose. I had to pretend that it didn't, and after a while the pretense became real." She frowned, creating a tiny cleft between her brows. "It still bothers me in the sense that someone has died, usually for very little reason, but seeing the body doesn't really bother me anymore. Besides, I always hope I'll discover something that will help solve the case."

"Maybe you should have gone into law enforcement." The words were out before he realized how ridiculous they were. Not even the uncivilized West was likely to put women on the police force.

She laughed, and the sound was so pleasant he couldn't help smiling. She seemed to take his remark as an intentional joke.

"No," she said after a moment. "I love to write the story." She leaned slightly toward him as if she were about to share a secret. He took the opportunity to lean toward her, too, close enough to smell a hint of lilac and scented soap against her skin. It was a provocative image he knew he should shake, but he savored it instead.

"I want to be famous," she said fervently. "To travel. To send my stories to the biggest newspapers in the country. All I need is one big story, one big break."

Her dark blue eyes were watching him levelly, as if to gauge his reaction to her confession. He guessed she didn't share her dream with very many people. He felt honored and more than a little sad that he wouldn't be around to watch her achieve it. "You'll do it," he said softly.

She sat back and smiled at him. He would have been content simply to gaze at her, but she spoke again. "Now. What's your story? Why are you, as you say, fascinated by death?"

Chapter Five

LV couldn't believe her luck! The ghost chaser was about to explain the truth behind his obsession with the supernatural. This could be the very information that made her story! She wondered how rude it would be to take notes.

"Well, it goes back to my mother. Or maybe my brother." He paused, as if trying to decide where his story should start. "I had a younger brother," he said finally, "five years my junior. When he was barely more than two, he died of a fever—pneumonia, I suppose. No one ever talked about it, and I was a child then myself."

LV nodded her sympathy, trying to contain her excitement in the face of such a sad opening. He was deep inside himself now, looking at his past, and the sorrow she read in his eyes made her want to reach out and touch his cheek. But that would break the spell. She sat quietly, waiting.

She heard a door down the hall open and close. Light footfalls sounded on the carpet-covered floor outside. LV ignored the sounds, concentrating on the good-looking man in front of her. Good-looking? When had she come to that conclusion? Fascinating, maybe, but—

"Alfie?"

The name was a tiny sob at her door. Before LV could turn her head in that direction, Brian was out of his chair. He threw open the door and gathered the little girl into his arms.

"Were you frightened, Katie?" he asked.

She shook her head, but her arms were wrapped around his neck, and she buried her face in his shoulder.

"I'm sorry," he murmured, stroking the child's back. "I shouldn't have left you alone so long."

LV wasn't sure when she moved toward the little scene, wanting somehow to be part of it. She felt an odd sense of envy and couldn't exactly explain why. Because the story she had been waiting for had been interrupted?

"Do you want to sleep in here while Daddy and I talk?" she asked, laying her hand on the small blond head.

Katherine raised her head, one stray tear

hovering on her eyelashes. "Daddy needs to sleep, too," she said.

LV wanted to argue. She wanted Brian to stay—to tell her his story, of course. No other reason.

"She's right," Brian said softly, his eyes meeting LV's. "I was up all night, and I'm just running on nerves now. And you have a story to write before the stage comes in this afternoon."

LV nodded reluctantly and watched him step through the still-open door, Katherine in his arms. He turned back toward her as if there was something he wanted to say. After a moment he nodded and turned toward his room.

LV closed the door and leaned her forehead against it. So close! She had been so close to insight into the strangest man she had ever met, and suddenly the opportunity was gone. Without his background she didn't have much of a story on her ghost chaser. The most she could do was mention him in her murder article. And even that was far from complete, though the third murder had made it somewhat more interesting.

And the little girl's story was far from finished, too. Would she get to stay with her new daddy? Would he leave her at an orphanage when he went home?

She pushed away from the door and turned her gaze to the cluttered table across the room.

There was only one decision that made any sense. She would not be on that stage this afternoon.

But an update on the murders would be. She hurried to the table, glancing at the watch that was pinned to her bodice. She had plenty of time to write the story, along with letters to her father and her boss.

After they were safely on the stage she would do a little clothes shopping. Armed with a new dress, she would get the story out of Brian. She closed her eyes, trying to call up the expression on his face as he'd begun his tale.

Instead she saw his gentle hand stroking the child's back and realized of whom she had been envious. *Well!* Wasn't that odd? She *was* actually attracted to the man. That hadn't happened since she was a silly schoolgirl. Why on earth would it be happening now?

It wasn't, she decided. She was on the verge of her big break, and her mind was playing tricks on her, mistaking excitement about a story for excitement about its subject. She didn't need a man, didn't want a man. What man was going to let his wife travel all over writing stories? So if she didn't want a man, she couldn't possibly be attracted to one. It would be like . . . like being attracted by a cup of coffee when you didn't even like coffee. *Impossible!*

Her subconscious was simply trying to remind her that there was more to her ghost chaser than wacky beliefs. He was also foolish enough to let a little girl call him Daddy and come to count on him when he would probably break the poor little thing's heart.

But even as she thought it, she couldn't quite believe he'd do anything to hurt Katherine. At least not intentionally. As for right now, the child was safe in his arms.

LV frowned. There was that odd spark of envy again.

Brian slept for several hours and woke to find Katie busily playing with her hair ribbons. He watched her for a moment as she wrapped one strand around a handful of others and tied a knot. Her tongue was caught between her teeth, and a frown creased her brow as she worked. He looked again at the tangled mess in her lap and tried to figure out what her plan might be. He couldn't guess. Maybe he didn't know enough about girls.

"Whatcha making?" he asked.

She jumped, evidence of her deep concentration, but recovered quickly. "I'm making a doll."

"Yeah?" He watched her for another long moment. "Why?"

The little girl dropped the ribbons and frowned at the mess, obviously unsatisfied with her creation. "I used to have a doll," she said softly. "My grandma made it. But I lost it sometime. On the train, I think. I thought I'd like a new one, but I don't know how to make one."

"Come here," Brian said, sitting up in the bed. He pulled Katie onto his lap and kissed her forehead. "Maybe someone with very clever hands could make a bunch of ribbons look a little like a doll, but I think there are better ways of making them."

"Do you know how?" she asked eagerly.

"Not me," he said. "But we can check some of the stores downtown. If they don't have dolls, we can find a seamstress. Every little girl should have a doll."

"Do you think Alfie can make one?" Katie asked eagerly.

"No," Brian said without a moment's hesitation. "But I bet she had one when she was little." He set her off his lap and swung his legs off the bed.

"Can she come help us find one?" Katie asked, running to bring Brian his shoes.

He used his shoes as an excuse to put off his answer. Somehow he had been picturing her along as they shopped. "She's got to write her story; then she's leaving this afternoon. What time is it, anyway?"

Katie ran to the table where he had left his watch and deftly popped the cover open. "The long hand's on the nine and the short hand's straight up. That's . . . the queen."

"Quarter till queen," Brian muttered. "It's almost noon. Are you hungry?"

Katie nodded vigorously. "I bet Alfie's hungry, too."

Brian cringed. If she was, she was perfectly capable of taking care of herself. It would be natural to invite her to join them, of course. But would spending one more meal with her make it easier to let her go? And why did it seem so difficult in the first place? He barely knew her.

Maybe it shouldn't be difficult, but it was. If he spent any more time with her he was liable to chase after her and beg her to stay.

"Let's just have lunch together, you and me. Then we'll find you a doll. After that, I've got a couple of letters to write before the stage gets here."

"And I'll be good while you write, 'cause I'll have a doll."

"Oh, you're good anyway," Brian said, snatching her up and tossing her on the bed. He ran to the table, grabbing his watch and wallet. "Race you to the door."

But she had seen it coming and was already off the bed. "I win," she crowed a moment before he caught up with her.

He opened the door. "I think you cheated."

"I think you cheated," Katie echoed, running ahead to the stairs.

Brian followed more slowly, resisting the urge to knock on Alfie's door as he went by.

LV heard a commotion below and glanced out her window. The stage! She wasn't sure how long it stayed in town before starting the long haul back down to Denver, but she absolutely had to have her article and the letters on board.

She scribbled the last line to her father, hoping he would heed her plea and send some money. She always traveled with emergency money beyond the paper's travel allowance, but it was going to disappear fast in this town of inflated prices. And she had no idea how long she would be here.

She came to her feet as she folded the letter, gathered the others, and headed for the door. Outside she found Brian talking to the driver. He stopped midsentence when he saw her. "Hello, Mr. Reed. Katherine." The little girl glanced up from where she sat on the edge of the boardwalk, but immediately returned her attention to a golden-haired doll in a bright blue dress.

"Alfie," Brian said. She should have known he wouldn't follow normal rules of protocol. But it wasn't enough to wipe the smile off her face. If fact it might have brightened slightly when she'd raised her eyes to his. But only accidentally.

"I have some letters to send with the stage," she said, recalling her errand. She stepped up to the driver and handed them over, finding herself that much closer to Brian.

"Just letters?"

"Yes. And the first article. I can't very well leave with the murders unsolved. Disappointed?" she asked, knowing by the light in his eyes that he was not, but wondering if he would admit it.

"Delighted," he said, making her catch her breath.

"Don't tell me you're here to see me off," she said, giving him a flirtatious smile. What had gotten into her? She wasn't really that pleased that he was here.

"I came to beg you to stay," he said, "in case there are any more bodies to examine."

She had to laugh. Except for his eyes, he had seemed quite serious. "I'm glad I could save you the trouble."

"Not to mention the humiliation," he said, then added, "I've written letters to my associates to look up Katie's family. I wanted to send them off as soon as possible."

"I see," she said, trying to convince herself that she hadn't been acting like a fool. She searched her mind for something else to say, something intelligent. Something that would put them back on their former footing, whatever that had been.

The stage driver had long since left them to themselves. No help there. Katherine was completely occupied with the doll.

While she was trying to think of something witty, Brian asked, "Have you had lunch?"

"I got a tray from the kitchen," she answered.

The silence descended again. Why did she feel so awkward? They were business associates, nothing more, thrown together by their mutual interest in a murder and a little girl. With that reminder, LV found it easier to ask, "Have you talked to the Indian yet?"

"I was going to try to find him this afternoon," he said, taking her elbow and leading her toward Katherine. "Want to come?"

"Of course," she said.

Katherine stood and joined them, taking Brian's hand. Instead of reentering the hotel, he walked them down the street. "His name is Willy Four Eyes," he explained. "I have directions to his place. It's up beyond the Winter's Gate Mine. There's supposed to be a wagon road up to it."

"Wonderful," LV said, remembering the narrow track that led to the mine. "What else do you know about him?"

"Not much. I understand he's had some education, but lives like a hermit." He led them into the livery, where their buggy was already waiting. In a few minutes they were aboard and moving out into the street.

"He probably lives in an abandoned mine," LV said, thinking aloud, "though most have vertical shafts rather than horizontal, like the Copper Kettle."

"Maybe he's actually found a natural cave," Brian suggested.

LV cast him a look over the top of Katherine's blond head. "If we're invited in, I think I'll pass."

He grinned at her. There was something very

charming about his grin. Maybe that was how he got away with being crazy. And he was crazy, she reminded herself, turning away. He not only believed in ghosts; he accepted the notion so completely that he expected those around him to accept it, too.

She had to find out why. What in his early upbringing had planted the notion in his impressionable mind, and why had he not outgrown it? She would have asked him, but she knew the story began with a child's death, and Katherine had certainly had enough death in her young life. She didn't need to hear about another one. Especially that of a child.

Still, the question burned in her brain all the way up the mountain. Had he seen his brother's ghost? Did he still see it? Did he smoke a little opium now and again to make the visions clearer?

She turned to look at his profile. He seemed a little too healthy to be an opium user. He was trim and not as muscular as men used to physical labor, but he didn't have the starved, pale look of the men she had seen after a raid on an opium den. She wondered if time was a factor.

He must have sensed her scrutiny, because his head turned in her direction. His deep brown eyes caught and held her gaze. His eyes, she decided, could make a woman believe in magic.

The thought startled her, and she managed to turn away.

"There's the mine," he said after a few minutes. "It shouldn't be too much farther."

"Good." Katherine sighed. "We're tired of jerking around. Linda wants to get out and play."

LV smiled. The road had gotten steadily rougher. "You named your doll Linda?" she asked, hoping to distract the child.

Katherine shrugged her shoulders. "I don't know. I'm just trying it out. Daddy suggested a bunch of names to try."

LV realized Brian was watching her. "Try some other ones," he said.

Katherine held the doll in front of her. "Does she look like a Laura or a Libby or a Lottie?" She turned her face up to LV.

"I don't know, sweetheart," she said.

Katherine turned toward Brian and LV did the same, only to discover him watching her closely. He shook his head briefly at Katherine. "Try Lisa or Loretta."

Katherine looked up at LV questioningly and realization dawned. They were trying to guess *her* name. She cast Brian a knowing smile and saw him accept defeat. "I'm sure you'll think of just the right name," she said.

Brian and Katherine exchanged a look, and LV couldn't resist a laugh. She was still chuckling when Brian hauled on the reins, bringing the buggy to a shaky stop.

"What is it?" she asked just before she saw it, a charming little cottage almost hidden by pines, rocks, and the natural lay of the land. "That can't be—"

"I think it is. Have you changed your mind about going inside?"

She didn't answer. The door had opened and a man stepped outside. He didn't look more than forty and was dressed like any of the miners they had seen in town, except for the glasses he wore. For a moment, LV was certain they had made a mistake. She opened her mouth to ask him for directions when the wind blew a lock of straight black hair over his shoulder.

"You folks lost?" He turned a warm smile toward Katherine.

"Willy Four Eyes?" Brian asked.

"Yes. What can I do for you?"

Katherine was the first to speak. "Can my dolly and me get out and play? We're tired of riding."

LV stared at her. What had happened to, "I'm not supposed to talk to strangers"?

"Certainly, young lady," Willy said, "if it's all right with your folks."

"We'd like to ask you a few questions," Brian said.

"About the murders," LV added. If they weren't welcome, she wanted to know it before they were out of the buggy.

"That is, if you don't mind," Brian said.

Willy looked from one to the other; then his eyes settled back on Katherine. "Come on inside. I'll make coffee." He reached for

Katherine to help her down, and she went eagerly into his arms. "When a family is investigating a murder, I have to assume they're related to one of the deceased."

"We're not a family," LV said quickly. Brian had just helped her out of the buggy, and the comment startled her enough that she forgot to step away once she was on the ground. And the only reason his hand lingered on the small of her back when she turned toward their host was because she was standing too close for him to do otherwise.

"I've been hired by Mr. Wingate," Brian said. "Miss Foster is—"

"—a reporter," she said, breaking contact so her brain would work again. She wasn't about to let Brian do all the talking.

"And the child?" Willy tipped his head toward Katherine, who had walked off a ways and was whispering to her doll.

"She's with me," Brian said.

Willy shook his head. "She looks more like Miss Foster."

"A coincidence," Brian said. "She's an orphan—"

"—but Brian's looking after her." LV didn't want Katherine to overhear and become concerned.

"Until I can find some family," Brian added.

Curiosity was evident in the dark eyes magnified behind the wire rims. "How long have you two worked together?"

How had it gotten turned around so that this Indian was asking all the questions? Of course, knowing the answers might put him at ease and make him more forthcoming. "We met yesterday," LV said.

"We're both working on the same case."

"So we're working together."

Willy chuckled. LV glanced at Brian. He seemed as confused as she was. "What's funny?" she ventured.

"I think you'll keep working together. The harmony's right." He started toward the house.

"Harmony?" LV and Brian asked together.

He turned. "You finish each other's sentences."

LV and Brian exchanged a look of chagrin before they followed him into his house.

The harmony was right? Oh, wonderful, LV thought, I work well with crazy people. Though she had to admit Brian didn't always seem crazy. Sometimes he seemed . . .

His hand was on the small of her back again as he let her precede him through the door. The casual touch made her forget what she was thinking. Or maybe it didn't. Maybe it simply confirmed what she was thinking. She found Brian attractive, but she could not let that make any difference. She had to write this story and his story without any emotional attachment.

Katherine had moved into the room with her and stood next to Brian. The little girl's story,

LV decided, would be written with as much emotion as she could muster.

First things first, she reminded herself. They were here for a reason. Willy had led them to a table near a small iron stove and was busy making coffee. The room was larger than she'd expected and filled with simple yet elegant furniture and an amazing amount of clutter ranging from books and what looked like surveyor's instruments to decorations that were purely Indian in origin.

As LV took the seat Brian held for her, she wondered who had built the house with its smooth wood floor and its hinged window sashes. There had to be a story of how the house had come into this hermit's possession. There was also a story behind the man's surprising command of English.

But she wasn't sure Brian was going to let her sit here and collect all that information. This man had been discovered standing over the bodies of two murdered miners. The townspeople had said he was harmless. She had therefore pictured him as aged. He wasn't. Therefore in her opinion, he should be considered a suspect.

Brian had taken a seat across from her and was looking around with at least as much curiosity as she was. She wondered if he read different things from their surroundings. Katherine had found a large chair draped with a fur robe and was whispering and growling at her doll as she climbed into it.

When the coffee was heating on the stove, Willy joined them at the table. "I assume you've heard that I was the first to find the bodies," he said, looking oddly self-conscious. "I figured it was only a matter of time before someone came to ask about that. Not that the town marshal has, by the way."

"Did you kill those men?" Brian asked, startling LV. If he had, she figured he would either deny it now or kill them all as well.

But Willy shook his head. "They were dead when I found them."

"Killed by the ghosts of your people." Brian said it as if it were an easily accepted statement. His eyes were on the Indian, waiting for his answer. LV knew what it was like to be pinned by those probing eyes.

Willy actually squirmed. "That was an impulsive statement, I admit. A nice thought, though," he added with a grin. "Sometimes I wish the white men would all go away."

"Would *you* kill them to make them go away?"

LV found herself hoping Brian was armed. His manner of interrogation seemed a little reckless, albeit fascinating.

Willy actually laughed. "If I thought killing a few would make the rest leave, I might at least give it some thought."

Willy got up to check the coffee and gather cups. When his back was turned, LV tried to catch Brian's eye, but he was still intent on Willy. "Have you given it some thought?"

He'll probably start with us. This was the last interview she was conducting with this man, if it wasn't her last interview ever.

"Not seriously," Willy said, bringing cups to the table. "For one thing, I know there are plenty more where these came from, and for another, I have to admit to being somewhat dependent on the town. I can't raise corn, let alone wheat up here, nor am I interested in keeping a milk cow. Cream?" He sat a small pitcher and a sugar bowl on the table.

"How do you get money for your purchases?"

Willy brought the coffee to the table, with his left hand, LV noticed with some relief, although that might not be conclusive. "I roll dead miners," he said and filled the cups. Looking up, he added, "That's a joke."

At least that shut Brian up for a moment.

"There aren't really any ghosts, are there?" LV asked.

"Oh, there are ghosts, Miss Foster. I see them in my dreams. I hear them scream and I watch them die." He took his seat again, having returned the coffeepot to the stove. "But those could be memories," he added, nodding. "Or maybe it's the same thing."

Something about the haunted look on his face convinced LV that Willy hadn't killed the two miners. She poured a little of the cream into her coffee to cool it faster and remembered Brian's last question. Before she repeated it, Brian asked another.

"What did you study in college, Mr. Tisdale?"

LV was glad her cup was only an inch above the saucer and that the coffee that sloshed out hadn't landed on her dress. "Tisdale?"

Willy seemed only mildly surprised.

"I assume the diploma is yours," Brian said, nodding toward the wall behind LV. She turned to see. The framed document was decorated with feathers and beads, but it was still recognizable.

"Architecture," Willy answered.

"Why don't you use your real name?" LV asked before it occurred to her that he might be wanted under his real name.

"One name's as real as the next. The Tisdales took me in as a child and gave me their name. Does that make it my real name? My people give each other many names. Which ones are real? The children at school called me Four Eyes. I supposed I respected their right to name me as much as my adoptive parents. My original name is lost from memory."

LV took a moment to digest this. "Is that how you earn a living?" she asked. "As an architect?"

Willy gave her a sad smile. "I might be able to if I lived someplace else, but the mountains called to me. No. Since the town built an opera house instead of a school, I find it possible to earn as much as I need teaching some of the children. It seems I'm the only one around with a college education who isn't bent on digging a fortune out of the ground.

"They brought in an architect from Denver for the opera house, by the way."

He looked both sad and resigned as he sipped his coffee, and LV would have respected the silence, but Brian asked another question. "Have you heard stories of the ghost at Winter's Gate Mine?"

LV rolled her eyes, but of course Brian didn't see it. Willy might have, though. She was so much better at interviews when she was on her own.

"Wingate's wife?" Willy asked. "Sure, I've heard about her. She's the favorite topic of my students, since they have to pass the mine to get here. I haven't spent any time looking for her, though. I have enough ghosts of my own."

Chapter Six

That, Brian thought, took care of the Indian ghosts. He was more convinced than ever of the existence of the Wingate ghost, however. What, if anything, it had to do with the deaths was another question.

They were making their way slowly back down the mountain. The horse seemed happy enough with the pace, though it could probably sense some impatience from one of his passengers.

He cast a quick glance at Alfie. She was on the downward side of this particular stretch of the hairpin road, and the town seemed far below her. He didn't let his gaze linger on her, though he would have liked to. If he didn't keep his attention firmly on the narrow track, it was easy to imagine them plunging down the rocky slope to the valley floor.

Brian wasn't sure whether Alfie's impatience was with the pace or with him. He knew she hadn't been particularly impressed with his style of questioning Willy. And she hadn't been pleased with the man's suggestion that they made a good team. *Displeased* didn't exactly describe his own feelings. *Alarmed* was more like it. He had already had a few thoughts along the same lines, but they centered more on pleasure than business.

It was ridiculous, of course. She thought he was crazy. Even if she didn't, she wasn't the type he could love, then leave behind. And he harbored no illusions of any permanent relationship. What woman would be willing to sit at home while he traveled all over studying ghosts? None, especially not Alfie. She had her own dreams.

Still, he intended to enjoy her company for as long as he could. Since there was no hope of making her fall in love with him, the insanity factor being what it was, he would have to settle for keeping her entertained.

"So," he began, resisting the urge to look in her direction until the horse had negotiated a sharp turn and put her on the uphill side again. "Want to try to see the ghost again tonight?"

Alfie's incredulous expression made him smile. "Guess not," he said.

"I seed the ghost last night, Daddy," Katie said. "I want to see the players."

"Players?"

Brian explained, "There's a troupe of actors in town that will be performing at the opera house this evening. They were putting up posters while we were shopping."

"I'm not sure that's an appropriate place to take a child," LV said.

Brian looked into Katie's upturned face. How could he deny her anything? "They called it entertainment for all ages," he said.

They had almost reached the valley, and Brian turned the horse onto the road that slanted down toward the business section of town. Discordant music could be heard from San Francisco Street.

"But in a town like this, things might get a little rowdy," Alfie warned.

Brian accepted the truth in that. Still . . . "She'll be all right. We can take care of her."

He wasn't sure she heard him. Her attention had been drawn to something, or someone, ahead. It didn't take long for Brian to discover what had caught her attention. Jason Wingate. Now why did he have a sudden urge to run the man over?

"I need to talk to him," Alfie said.

"Who?" Brian asked, pretending—hoping—he didn't know.

"Jason. Could you stop here?"

Brian considered refusing, claiming it wasn't

safe in the traffic, which seemed unfortunately light at the moment. But she had turned toward him when she spoke, and even as he debated he was hauling back on the reins.

"Thanks," she said. "I'll talk to you later." She hopped out of the buggy before it had completely stopped, or so it seemed, and stepped onto the boardwalk.

"Later," Brian murmured.

Wingate had evidently seen her as well, and came out to meet her. They looked pleased to see each other and started down the street together. "He's a little young for her, don't you think?" Brian muttered.

Katie looked up at him. "Where's she going?"

Brian shook his head. "I don't know. But don't worry. She can take care of herself."

He believed it. He really did. And he wasn't jealous of the young Wingate. He was simply disappointed. "We'll have fun, just the two of us," he said, as much to himself as to Katie.

He moved the buggy back into the street. Moments before he turned in at the livery, a cloud blocked the sun. The temperature seemed to drop several degrees. It looked as though they were in for a shower. Funny, he hadn't noticed the clouds until Alfie had left.

After settling the bill, he helped Katie out and started toward the hotel. He wanted to look back and see if Alfie was coming toward them, but he knew the street was curved enough that he probably wouldn't see her. And certainly if he could see her, she could see him.

Katie tugged on his hand and he stopped.

"We should wait for Alfie," she said.

Hell, yes, and blame it on Katie if she doesn't like it. But did he really want to see her walking with Wingate?

"She's a grown woman," Brian said. "She can find her way to the hotel."

"But she left this in the buggy." Katie held up a small lady's bag, one he had seen Alfie carrying.

He took half a second to take the imminent rain into consideration. "Let's go meet them," he said.

They made their way through the other pedestrians, and after about a block Brian could see them ahead. Alfie's hand was tucked in the crook of Wingate's arm and held possessively close to his side. He was talking. She was listening intently. Smiling. He almost hated to interrupt them. Almost.

Katie broke away from him, running ahead. "Alfie!" the little girl shouted. Brian followed more slowly.

Alfie knelt to the child's level as she ran toward her. She didn't look nearly as annoyed as Brian thought she might. But then, she hadn't turned her attention to him yet.

Alfie straightened to say something to Wingate. After a moment Wingate swaggered off the way he had come. Brian watched Alfie and Katie, their hands clasped together, move in his direction. Why were they such a pleasing sight? Pleasing beyond the simple fact that they were both pretty.

They met him before he had time to ponder the question.

"We found her," Katie said, looking immensely relieved.

"You shouldn't wander off like that," he said.

Alfie gave him a pained look and started toward the hotel. He fought a grin as he fell in beside her. "What did you and Junior find to talk about?" he asked.

"He invited me to dinner," she said, looking straight ahead.

"At the hotel dining room," Katie supplied. "At seven."

Half a block from the hotel Alfie stopped. "I have some shopping to do," she said. "I'll see both of you later." She knelt and gave Katie a kiss on her cheek. "Thanks for bringing my purse," she said.

In a moment she had slipped inside the shop. A dress shop. She wanted to be pretty for her date.

Brian looked down at Katie. She was looking sadly at the door, hurt to be left out of LV's plans.

"How do you like that?" he said with mock indignation. "I was returning her purse, too."

Katie giggled. "Daddy wanted a kiss."

"I'd rather have one from you, anyway." He swung her into his arms, and she kissed his cheek. "How about a hug to go with that?"

"That better?"

"All better. Now what do you suppose we should do?" He carried the little girl toward the hotel.

"I think I want to shop in that store." She pointed over his shoulder.

"Shop for what?"

"I want to look at . . . " She craned her neck to see behind them. " . . . a dress. Yes, a dress."

"I think we'd better leave Miss Alfie alone for now," Brian said, knowing he was far too tempted by the suggestion.

"Is she mad at us?"

At Katie's worried expression, Brian laughed. "She isn't mad at you, anyway. You got a kiss."

She took his face between her tiny hands. "She didn't kiss you 'cause you're scratchy."

"I thought girls liked scratchy," he said, trying to maneuver his face so he could rub it against hers.

Katie squealed so loudly that he was sure Alfie must have heard.

Most of the store's supply of ready-made dresses seemed to be of a somewhat flamboyant style. Considering the female population of the town, LV decided that wasn't surprising. She did find a couple of skirts and bodices that were a little more conservative, and one lovely green dress that was just on the edge of propriety.

The shopkeeper didn't seemed disposed to start a line of credit for her so she counted her money and debated. The skirts would make more sense as she continued her investigation. But the dress would be more appropriate for this evening. Jason seemed intent on flirting with her, and going along seemed the best way to encourage him to talk. Besides, she would enjoy dressing up after two days in her work clothes.

The shopkeeper assured her that the few alterations would be completed during the next hour, and LV went off in search of the local excuse for the law. She didn't expect to get any information out of Hagman, but he might let her see the body. She'd like to take a closer look under a little more light.

LV was surprised to find Marshal Hagman actually in his office. Of course, his feet were propped up on his desk and he was sleeping. She let the door slam behind her a little harder than necessary. The pressure blew long-dormant dust into the air to mix with the smell of smoke and sweat.

Hagman jumped, nearly knocking over his tipped-back chair. He caught his balance and scowled at LV.

She smiled sweetly. "I'm so sorry, Marshal. Did I wake you?"

"No, of course not, little lady. I was puzzling out this here rash of murders we got."

"Any theories?"

"Well, now, why would I want to share with you?" He came to his feet and started slowly around his desk, grinning suggestively.

"Because I'll tell you what I find when I examine this latest body."

She watched the grin turn to mild disgust. "I mighta knowed you'd be around askin' to see it. You go on over to the undertaker's. Tell 'im I gave you the go-ahead."

LV thanked him and exited the office quickly, taking in a deep breath of crisp air once she was outside. The undertaker was almost next door to the jail. She stepped inside just as a spattering of raindrops began to fall. She was greeted by a middle-aged woman who hadn't been there the day before.

"The marshal gave me permission to see the body," she said.

"Are you kin?" she asked kindly.

"A reporter," LV said. She was already preparing herself to see the body and didn't realize how curt her answer was until she saw the startled look on the woman's face.

"Well," she said hesitantly, "if you have permission."

"Thank you," LV said, trying for a gentler tone.

With skeptical look, the woman led LV to the

back room where she had gone the day before. The first two bodies had been removed. There was one shroud-draped table. LV forced herself to relax, to do what she had to do.

"My husband hasn't cleaned him up yet," the woman said behind her, startling her.

"Good," LV said. She stepped forward and moved the sheet aside.

While LV dressed for dinner she had to keep reminding herself that she wasn't going to be eating with Brian. She was going to spend the evening with Jason, fishing for information. This dress, with all the drapes of fabric on the bottom and a surprising lack of fabric on top—this dress that was alarmingly difficult to walk in—was bait.

This was what she had come here for, to find out about the murders, to write her story, and Jason might tell her something when they were alone that he wouldn't have in his father's presence. The only reason she thought about Brian at all was because he was also a story, and a more compelling one than these senseless murders.

The Ghost Chaser. That would be her headline. How had the death of a brother warped his young mind, sent him off on this insane quest? What unusual things had he witnessed that reaffirmed his belief? How could a person be both charming and insane?

She shook her head. She was actually smiling! "Because it's a great story," she said firmly.

She went back to fixing her hair with fresh determination. She was going to be late arriving downstairs. Making Jason wait a few minutes wasn't necessarily a bad idea, but when she arrived she had to make him think she had been worth the wait.

The dining room was approximately half-full when LV entered. Jason stood immediately, as if he thought she would have trouble finding him. He watched her with open admiration as she made her way toward him. Her necessarily slow steps were good for something, she decided, though she had to hope the place didn't catch on fire.

"You look lovely," he said as he held her chair.

"Thank you. You look rather dashing yourself." She gave him her warmest smile and even risked a light touch to the sleeve of his well-cut suit as he sat down. She had to be careful. There was flirting and then there was flirting. She didn't know this man.

"I took the liberty of ordering for us both," he said, pouring her a glass of red wine. "I hope you don't mind."

"Of course not." When had she ever really cared what she ate? "I'm curious, Jason. Since your father's mine is closed, what do you find to do all day?"

"The place needs to be guarded from looters. The men we hire to do it don't last long." There was an odd lack of interest in his voice.

"I'd think the ghost would scare away any thieves," she said brightly.

Jason chuckled. "My father doesn't think we should count on that."

"Tell me about your father," she suggested.

"Are we going to talk about the mine and my father all evening?"

Darn. She smiled apologetically. "I'm sorry. A reporter's habit, I guess."

Their dinners arrived.

And so had Brian and Katherine, LV noticed with some discomfort. They took a table across the room, with Brian facing her. He gave her a slight nod, then turned his attention to Katherine. She was dressed in another of her pretty dresses, and her hair was tied at the nape of her neck with a bright blue bow. Brian had done a nice job of brushing her hair and tying the ribbon. She would have left the tails of the ribbon a little longer, perhaps, to keep the bow from looking quite so large on the little head.

"You don't mind if I call you LV, do you?"

She only half heard Jason. Was she hurt that Brian hadn't asked her to fix Katherine's hair? *How silly.*

"Miss Foster?"

"Alfie," she muttered before catching herself. "Of course you may call me LV. We're friends, aren't we?"

"I think I lost you there for a minute." He sounded a little hurt.

"Reporters," she said lightly, then looked down at her plate. "Oh, this looks lovely. Could you pass the salt?"

It shouldn't be any more difficult to quiz Jason with Brian across the room. He couldn't hear her. He didn't care if she was here with another man. He wouldn't be jealous if he saw her flirting.

Or would he? What a deliciously wicked thought. Without analyzing why the prospect of making Brian jealous was in any way appealing, she turned her sweetest smile on Jason.

"It's really nice of you to take me to dinner," she said. "So often when I come into a town to do a story, I make only enemies." She would have tried to look pouty, but it wasn't part of her repertoire.

"Perhaps that's because other men are afraid of you."

"Afraid! Of me? Or afraid of my pen?"

He laughed. "Your pen, perhaps. But also of you. Women who are so self-reliant intimidate some men. They feel less necessary."

Alfie knew the truth in that but pretended to be surprised. "But you aren't afraid?"

"Perhaps I'm smarter than the others. Or braver."

She took a sip of wine to hide her grin. My, my, what a big head this young man had. She was becoming bored with the exchange. And it wasn't because she had just heard the faint sound of laughter from across the room and recognized Brian's voice.

It was because this stupid conversation wasn't getting her anywhere. "I already knew you were brave," she said, hoping she wasn't overdoing it. "Not many men are willing to stay on that mountain with the ghost."

She kept forgetting to eat, but he was making major inroads into his steak, and she had to wait for him to answer. "You don't believe in the ghost," he stated.

She forced a smile. "Why do you think that? Nearly everyone in town is at least willing to accept the possibility."

"They're ignorant and bored. A ghost is entertaining."

"I see. And the murders?"

He grinned at her. "There you go being a reporter again. Murder isn't a subject for polite conversation. I'd rather talk about you. Why would such a pretty girl want to do a man's job?"

Alfie sighed. Her own history was the last thing she was interested in discussing. She told him a little about her background with the paper, using the food in front of her as an excuse for occasional silences, hoping he would fill them with something that could lead her back to the subjects she wanted him to discuss. No luck. Finally she told him about her father, the former mayor, and her mother, the activist, and saw an opening.

"What about your mother?" She hoped the question sounded innocent.

"She died when I was a boy," he said. Alfie thought a shadow crossed his face, but it was quickly gone. "I barely remember her. Didn't you know?" he asked, leaning closer. "She's the ghost."

"Then you do believe in it," she said quickly, hoping to cover the fact that she had indeed heard that rumor. She leaned closer to him so he could smell her perfume. She tried for a husky whisper. "Have you seen her?"

He shook his head slowly. "Though, for you, my dear, I'd happily camp out on the mountain to wait for her to appear. Provided, of course, that you were waiting with me."

What a revolting prospect, she thought. "But that's how poor Mr. Trebly died. He was watching for the ghost."

He drew back. "What gave you that idea?" He returned his attention to his dinner, but she was sure she could detect some nervousness.

"Earlier that night he had talked to Mr. Reed." She had almost called him her partner. He was hardly that. She glanced across the room and found him watching her. She went on quickly. "They were going to meet up there on the mountain."

Jason was silent for a moment. When he turned back to her his smile was in place. "I think you're being too much of a reporter again. I really don't want to talk about the ghost or the murders."

"But everyone else is talking about them," she insisted.

"You can talk to everyone else tomorrow." He refilled her wineglass. "Tonight you're here with me, and I don't want to spend the whole evening talking about such morbid things. Did I tell you I've got tickets to the theater tonight?"

"How lovely," Alfie said, unwilling to accept defeat. She would try the indirect approach. If she flirted and teased and listened very carefully, maybe he'd say something that would give her insight into his father or the mine. She looked into his pale gray eyes and gave him what she hoped passed for an encouraging smile. The next moment she was reaching for the wineglass. It would be so much easier if he would simply answer her questions.

Brian hated to leave while Alfie was still throwing herself at the Wingate boy. Somehow it wasn't behavior he had expected from her. All through dinner he had tried to remind himself that she was after information, but that wasn't what it looked like from across the room. And it had gotten worse as the evening passed. By the time Katie had finished her dinner, Alfie seemed practically in Wingate's lap.

But he had to leave. He had arranged for box seats for Katie and himself to put them literally above the fray at the theater. He wanted to get Katie safely into the box before the crowd arrived.

He helped the little girl out of her chair and took her hand. "Daddy, I want to ask Alfie to come with us," she said as they started toward the door.

"I think Alfie has other plans."

"But maybe she'd rather be with us."

Brian took one last look at the pair in the corner. Alfie was smiling up at Wingate, her hand resting familiarly on his arm. He was telling her something that seemed to enthrall her. "I'm sure she would," he muttered, seeing Katie through the door.

They had brought their coats down when they came and left them in the lobby. He helped Katie into hers, crouching in front of her to see that it was buttoned. "Why the sad face?" he asked. "Do you want to go back to the room to get your doll?"

"Doesn't Alfie like us anymore?"

"How could she not like us?" he asked, hoping his grin was convincing. "We like us, don't we? We can't both be wrong."

That logic finally brought a smile to her face. Before he could come to his feet, she threw her arms around his neck. "I love you, Daddy."

"I love you, too, Katie," he murmured against the soft cheek. "We'd better hurry."

He hoped that explained why he had to pull away. Now would probably be a good time to remind the little girl that the current arrangement was temporary. He was only her daddy until her other relatives were found. What he needed, he supposed, was someone to remind *him.* He was starting to imagine taking her home with him, making room for her in the odd little house he had inherited from his uncle.

What did he think he would do when he had another case like this one? Pull her out of school to go along? Hire a housekeeper to look after her while he was gone? The damnedest thing was that neither solution seemed impossible. He could, quite easily, make room for her in his life.

Of course, all those fantasies seemed to include Alfie. That was how he knew they were fantasies. Alfie was not going to give up her dreams to fit into his. He would never ask that of her.

Alfie suppressed a sigh of relief when Jason finally decided it was time to head for the theater. Brian and Katherine had left several minutes earlier. She had tried to pretend she hadn't noticed, that she hadn't been aware of their voices as they talked softly, lingering just beyond the dining-room doors.

And why would she rather be with them? The man was crazy, and she had never liked the company of children. Perhaps the fault was with her current companion. She gave Jason an encouraging smile as he helped her into her wrap.

"I feel like the luckiest man in Glitter Creek," he whispered into her ear.

Alfie wanted to brush at her ear the way she would shoo away an insect. As soon as he wasn't looking she did it, just so that her ear would feel normal again. What a dreadfully long evening this was becoming. If only she could get him to talk about the mine.

Jason opened the door and held it for Alfie. As she stepped onto the boardwalk, she found her way blocked by the elder Mr. Wingate.

"Excuse me, Miss . . . Forest, is it?"

"Foster," she said. He had stepped away to allow room on the boardwalk for her and Jason. There was surprise on the older man's face when he realized who her companion was.

"Good evening, Father," Jason said, his voice chillier than the mountain air.

Wingate snorted. "It was until now. Though I suppose I should be happy to see you with a woman who at least pretends at respectability."

"Let's go, LV," Jason said, taking her arm and giving his father a wide berth.

"What was he talking about?" Alfie asked, more curious than insulted, though she knew what Wingate had implied. A woman who traveled alone, doing what most thought was a man's job, was certain to have her virtue questioned from time to time. She didn't much care, at least not from Wingate. What she wanted to know was why father and son were so hostile.

"He didn't mean anything," Jason said, hurrying her down the boardwalk as if he thought his father might follow. "He's just a bitter old man."

"Why is he so bitter?" If he kept her walking this fast she was likely to fall. Stupid, hobbling styles! She pulled on Jason's arm, hoping to slow him down.

"Because he's old and jealous of my youth, I suppose. But then, I can't remember when he was ever any different."

"Poor Jason," Alfie cooed. "Life can have such burdens."

"It's not important," Jason said, turning on his charm again. "I hope you enjoy the show. Glitter Creek has quite an opera house. As beautiful as anything in Denver, I think."

Darn.

The theater was as lovely as Jason had promised. Alfie stepped into the hall and stood for a moment gazing around her. She wasn't looking at the ornately carved moldings or the gilt paint. She was looking for Brian.

He and Katherine occupied a box to the left of the stage. Brian was pointing out something to Katherine. Alfie wished she knew what it was that he shared with the child. When the girl nodded up at Brian and he smiled down at her, Alfie looked away. The wave of longing was entirely inappropriate.

She followed Jason to their seats and tried

to concentrate on the series of skits, recitals, and musical numbers. Though she tried not to look up at the box again, throughout the show she was conscious of their presence. And their distance.

Chapter Seven

"I hate for the evening to end so soon," Jason said for the fourth time.

"It doesn't seem early to me," Alfie said, barely hiding her impatience. "I was up early working on my story." Not to mention out half the night. She really was tired. Mostly, though, she was tired of Jason.

He had offered to buy her a drink at an establishment he swore was respectable. When she had feigned shock, he had offered to buy a bottle and bring it to her room, as if that were more appropriate. Next he had suggested a drive by moonlight, though there was no moon that Alfie could see.

Now she was standing in the hotel lobby

with her hand caught between the banister and Jason's palm. He was still hoping for an invitation upstairs. Of course, she bore some of the blame for that; she had led him on all evening. But she no longer had any expectations of extracting information from him. Even if she did, she wasn't willing to pay that price.

"It's been lovely, Jason," she said, trying for sweetness. "Perhaps I'll see you tomorrow."

"Don't I get a kiss good night?"

She had gone up one step before making the mistake of turning to say good night and thence getting her hand caught under his. Even so, she was several inches shorter than he was. She considered refusing, wondering if he would give in graciously or become angry. She decided for the sake of saving time simply to kiss him. What difference did it make? She had been cozying up to him all evening.

She had hoped for a quick peck and escape. Jason had other ideas. His free hand, the one that wasn't imprisoning hers, caught the back of her head and pulled her closer. Fortunately Alfie still had one unoccupied hand and used it to push against his chest. At least it kept a little space between them.

Jason's tongue was trying to force its way between Alfie's lips when he suddenly pulled away. She realized she had heard someone behind her, but, not expecting help, had dismissed it.

Jason made his departure rather quickly, with a terse "Good evening" to the person behind her. Once he was out the door and Alfie could breathe easily again, she turned to go up the stairs. Brian was several steps above her, watching her with those penetrating, unreadable eyes.

"What are you doing here?" She realized it was a stupid question. He was staying in the hotel, too. Was she hoping he'd say he was worried about her and was heading out to look for her?

"Katie wants some warm milk," he said, moving down the stairs.

He was past her before she realized she hadn't thanked him. In fact, he might even suppose she regretted the interruption. *What did she care?* she wondered as she watched him disappear into the dining room. She didn't want to get entangled with Brian any more than she did with Jason.

With that thought firmly in mind, she headed for her room. When the door was safely closed behind her, she leaned against it and groaned. What a horrible evening! A long, boring, frustrating evening. The possibility that Jason was frustrated, too, although in a different way, entered her mind. It made her feel worse. She had used him, teased him really. For a story.

"Well, darn it," she muttered, straightening. "It was for a *story*." She felt better already. In fact, she felt like discussing her findings, such as they were, with Brian. And in the process she could explain.

In case he cared.

Which he probably didn't.

But she'd do it anyway. She turned to reopen the door when she caught a glimpse of herself in the mirror. She'd change first, she decided. And wash. Definitely wash. She could still feel Jason on her skin.

Brian was pacing. Katie had drunk her milk and nodded off to sleep with a smile on her face. Brian had intended to spend some time reviewing what he knew, which wasn't much, and outlining what was yet to be done.

Wingate wanted proof that there was no ghost so he could hire miners again. Brian believed there *was* a ghost, which he wanted very much to see. Proving her existence was another matter, and would not make Wingate happy, though Brian found the prospect extremely exciting.

But here he was with a little girl in his care. Trebly's death had made the danger they faced all the more immediate. He couldn't leave Katie alone to go looking for the ghost. He couldn't take her with him again.

Part of him wondered how he had gotten himself into this sort of entanglement. The rest of him believed it was the best thing that had ever happened to him. How wonderful was a child's love! Her Aunt Candy was even more of a fool than he had first thought, and now he wished he had never called the girl to her attention. What if the woman changed her mind and decided she wanted Katie?

He walked to the bed and gazed down at the child. Asleep, with her lips parted and her inquisitive eyes closed, she looked more like a baby. He grinned. She was clever, though. What fun it would be to watch her slowly turn into a woman. A woman who could think for herself, with the courage to march off after her own dreams. A woman like Alfie.

He paced back toward the window. There were lights visible in several of the buildings across the street. A block away, the saloons would be busy—busy with customers he should be interviewing.

Would Jason have headed down there after leaving Alfie? Had he told her anything helpful? Had she even bothered to ask? Would she have taken him up to her room if she hadn't been caught?

Why did he find that thought so depressing? He had always thought that women should have the same rights as men, and though it was rather radical thinking, that should extend to sex, as well. If Alfie found a lover every time she left home in pursuit of a story, that was no different from a lot of men he knew. But somehow, thinking it was fair and seeing it happen were two different things.

Or maybe it was just because the woman in question was Alfie.

When the knock sounded on his door he knew who it was. Perhaps he had been half-conscious of movement in the next room, the closing of the door, footsteps in the hall. Or maybe it was because he wanted it to be Alfie.

She breezed past him when he opened the door.

"I didn't get you up, did I? I saw the light, but I thought maybe Katherine needed it to sleep." She spoke quickly, but softly.

She was wearing the high-necked blouse and the dark skirt again. It seemed almost prudish compared to what she'd worn for Jason. But then, she wasn't interested in flirting with Brian.

He closed the door and took his time turning back toward her. He didn't want her to sense his disappointment. In her? In himself for not being able to compete with men like Jason? He wasn't sure.

She was sitting in one of the chairs by the table when he finally faced her. "No, I was up," he said, though that was obvious by now.

"I just needed to talk to you. I hope you don't mind. We're not going to wake Katherine, are we?"

"I think she's a pretty sound sleeper." He took the chair across the table from her. "How was your evening?" He might as well get it over with.

She made a sound that could have been a groan. And it could have meant anything. "How did Katherine like the show?"

"I think she had fun. She missed you." He probably shouldn't have added that.

Alfie smiled. "She did? Isn't that sweet? I wished I'd been with you, too. I mean, with you and Katherine."

He nodded. Of course that was what she meant.

"The only thing I got out of Jason," she continued, "was the fact that he and his father don't get along."

"That and dinner and a show." Now why was he feeling sorry for Jason? Because in his place, he'd feel sorry for himself.

"I'm a terrible person, aren't I?"

She probably expected him to disagree. Not that he didn't. He was hurting just enough that he didn't feel like trying to make her feel better. Actually, he was a little relieved to find she felt some remorse.

"Why don't the two Wingates get along?" he asked.

"You mean, besides the fact that Dale Wingate is a pigheaded boor? I don't know."

Brian had to smile. Trust Alfie to lay it on the line.

Alfie spoke again after a moment of silence. "I examined Trebly's body today."

Brian felt a twinge, a queasiness in his gut. "Did you learn anything?"

She shook her head. "Knifed like the others. But something occurred to me."

She turned toward him. Half of her face was lit by the low-burning lamp, the other by the feeble light coming through the window. It ruined the symmetry of her face but made her look more beautiful. Or maybe less beautiful but more accessible. "What occurred to you?" he whispered.

"No one's trying to solve the murders. You're investigating a ghost. I'm just interested in a story."

"That's the town marshal's job, not ours," he said, feeling chastened nonetheless.

"He isn't doing it."

"And that seems to sit just fine with the townspeople."

She tapped a finger on her lower lip. It drew his instant attention. He hadn't noticed how perfectly those lips were shaped, how eminently kissable they were. Suddenly it didn't seem at all out of line to lean toward her and taste those lips.

But unfortunately, or perhaps fortunately, the table was in the way. And that physical obstacle was enough to bring him to his senses. That and the sound of her voice.

"Maybe to some, but we haven't exactly been interviewing the pillars of the community. I'm sure they don't like murders going unsolved in their town."

Brian stood and paced a few feet away. In

another minute the table might not be enough of an obstacle. "Who *are* the pillars here, Alfie? Everyone seems to be out to make a fortune, either off the mountains or off the miners. They built an impressive opera house, but there's no school except Willy Four Eyes's. The dominant business is the sale of alcohol. I think that the general feeling is every man for himself."

Alfie nodded in agreement. She had turned toward him. Her face and hair caught the glow of the lantern. He wondered if she had any idea of the picture she made. Considering her behavior with young Wingate, she probably did. He needed to remember that.

"Well," she said with a sigh, "I suppose you're right."

She looked as if she was about to go, which would probably be a very good thing. Even as he found himself breathing a little easier, his mind was searching for a reason for her to stay.

"I should go," she said.

Wait! It was on the tip of his tongue to say it aloud, but he hadn't thought of a reason yet.

"Unless . . . " she began.

Unless! Yes! Unless what?

" . . . you wanted to finish the story about your brother."

Perfect! God, he had almost said that aloud, too. He wasn't used to being affected by women in this way. Actually, he wasn't used to women sticking around once they learned he believed in ghosts.

As he walked back toward the table he couldn't help but ask himself why Alfie was still around. She would certainly agree with the others in their assessment of his sanity. He decided not to let the question spoil this time with her.

"I told you my brother died when he was two," he began, settling into the chair and giving himself a good view of her beautiful face. "I wanted to tell you about it so you'd understand . . . why I'm 'crazy.' "

She answered his grin with one of her own. "I've been curious."

He nodded, gradually turning serious as the events of his childhood came back to him. "It was very hard on my mother," he said softly. "As a child I couldn't quite understand why I wasn't enough for her. It was selfish, I suppose, but her grief hurt me."

"It wasn't selfish; it was childish," she said gently. "You were only seven."

It was foolish to be so touched by her understanding. Here he was wanting to kiss her again. "At any rate," he went on, pulling his gaze away from her face and settling it on a knot in the tabletop, "she slowly came out of her grief. At least that's what we thought. Then a few years later, she reported seeing my brother's ghost.

"At first my father said she was still grieving. I was told never to mention this ghost to anyone. Mother, however, wasn't a bit reticent on the subject. Eventually everyone knew that she saw ghosts. Father was mortified. He made excuses for her for a while, then threatened to have Mother committed. By this time I was old enough to raise a considerable protest. Father left us, but honestly, I hardly noticed. Mother died four years ago, of loneliness, I suppose."

"Did you ever see the ghost?"

Brian shook his head. "I didn't love him enough, I suppose. I hadn't really gotten to know him. He was little more than a baby, and I'm afraid I had thought of him as an intruder."

"Do you feel guilty about that?"

Brian looked up. The softly spoken question was more insightful than he wanted to admit. "The house I grew up in, where Mother saw the ghost, had belonged to my father's family. He let Mother and I live there until she died; then he moved back in. By then, he thought I was crazy, too, so I moved out. I wonder sometimes about the ghost, or maybe ghosts, that might still reside in that house."

"You left him alone with the ghosts?" There was no smile on her face, but there was certainly one in her voice.

"Not exactly," he said. "His wife and my four little half siblings live there with him."

"Do I sense a little resentment?"

"You're an insightful woman," he said, giving her an appraising look. "His wife is my age. I won't call her Mother."

She tried to hide her laughter behind her hand.

"This isn't supposed to be a funny story," he said, feeling a smile threaten his own lips.

"I know. And it isn't, really. Tell me about the 'considerable protest' that kept your mother out of an institution."

"I was aware of some . . . indiscretions that would have turned a divorce pretty nasty. He agreed to go quietly."

In the silence that followed, Brian reflected on what he had said. It hadn't explained things quite the way he had hoped. Alfie's next words confirmed his assessment.

"So you want to prove there are ghosts to vindicate your mother and spite your father."

"No." He rested his arms on the table and leaned toward her. "Can't you understand my fascination? I lived all those years in the presence of that ghost."

"Which you never saw."

"Which I never saw but know existed. My mother *wasn't* crazy."

"Grief-stricken to the point of deluding herself, perhaps?"

Brian pulled away from her. He hadn't really expected her to understand, had he? "Well, now you know why I'm crazy."

"I don't think you are."

He studied her eyes but couldn't determine whether she really meant it. "Thanks," he said tentatively.

"Eccentric as hell, but probably not crazy."

He forced a light laugh that wasn't meant to sound real.

She leaned across the table toward him, a move that had him mentally measuring the width of the table and the distance to her lips. "Do you know what else I think?"

He braced himself. "I'm sure you'll tell me."

"I think you can't accept death. That's why you believe in ghosts and that's why you're so squeamish even talking about dead bodies."

"No, that's where you're wrong," he said, moving forward to copy her pose. Her mouth was only inches away.

"Being squeamish of dead bodies is normal."

"Are you saying *I'm* not normal?" She managed to shorten the distance by about an inch and a half.

"I'm saying you're eccentric as hell." He hadn't meant for his voice to drop to such a seductive level. The table was cutting into his stomach, but he moved in another inch.

"Yeah?" Her voice had dropped, too.

"Most definitely." If he were a ghost, he'd go right though the damn table.

"Then why do you want to kiss me?"

"That's a good question. I suppose you have the answer."

"No, I just have another question." She was whispering now. His blood was swiftly leaving his brain for parts farther south. Without realizing it, he had started to come to his feet in order to bridge the last of the distance between them.

"Which is?" How could a couple of inches seem so far?

"Why don't you do it?"

Those perfect lips were against his before she had finished the question. They were every bit as soft and warm as he had imagined. And twice as responsive. In fact, her warm little tongue was between his lips before he had even considered taking such liberties. Why would she be so eager to kiss him? The answer hit him like a bucket of cold water: a story.

He broke away before he realized how disappointing it would be. He had been wanting to kiss her all evening, and now he was pulling away because he couldn't believe that she'd wanted it, too.

"What's wrong?" she asked.

She looked a little dazed. He wanted to believe it was real, but was hardly willing to trust his heart. He had no illusions about his own appeal, and she had already turned down Jason Wingate because he had no information for her. What information did Miss L. V. Foster want from him?

"The table," he said by way of explanation. It was cutting rather deeply into his thighs, though he had only just become aware of it.

Alfie took a deep breath and let it out slowly between pursed lips. Warm, delicious, hungry lips.

"I suppose I should go," she said.

"I suppose you should," he agreed, though that was the last thing he wanted. He wanted his brain to stay the hell out of the situation.

She didn't move and he was afraid to. Without the table between them, he wasn't sure what he would do. No, that wasn't true. He knew exactly what he would do.

"I'll see you tomorrow?" she asked.

"I'm sure you will."

"Good night, then."

"Good night."

He stood where he was until she had left his room, then sank slowly into the chair. Maybe he should have taken what she offered, regardless of her reasons. Maybe he could have had her without falling in love with her. But if that kiss was a preview of what the rest would be like, he doubted it. In fact, he was already more than half in love with her.

He chuckled at the silliness of his own thoughts. How did one measure love? If he was half in love, would she break only half his heart? And how would he feel about reading her story about him? Would it hurt more, the more he was in love? Less because she got the information for only one kiss?

He sat for a long time thinking about Alfie, her story, and his own pride. The only thing that cheered him up was picturing his father's reaction to Alfie's story.

* * *

Alfie took off her shoes so that she could pace her room without worrying that Brian would hear her. The last thing she wanted was for him to think his kiss or his dismissal had bothered her in any way. In fact, she would have loved to have convinced herself that she had been unmoved by either.

She had gone to his room for information. Now she had the foundation for a story on him. That was all she wanted. She should be ecstatic. If she couldn't sleep, she should be writing the story.

She shouldn't be mooning over someone she hadn't even thought was handsome when she'd first seen him. Though, she decided, he did have an interesting face. Captivating eyes, that was certain. And the rest, well, perhaps it was the familiarity. No, it was more than that.

"It's a beloved face," she whispered. She put her hands over her mouth as if that would stop the thought, send it back from whence it came. But it was too late. The thought had been spoken and her heart had agreed. Was she in love with Brian Reed, eccentric investigator specializing in supernatural phenomena?

With a sigh, she slid her hands away from her mouth, letting her fingers linger a moment on her lips. He had wanted to kiss her; she was sure of it. She was familiar with the warm spark of desire in a man's eyes, with his shift of interest from the conversation to her lips.

What was unfamiliar was her own response

to it. She could have played with him a while, gotten some more information, then coolly walked away. Or at least she could have with any other man. With Brian, she had practically begged him to kiss her. And when he had, she had wanted to devour him.

Which might have been why he pulled away. That or the recollection of the kiss that he had witnessed on the stairs. Men were funny about presampled goods, even when kisses were all that was involved.

The thought made her feel depressed. The stupid kiss she had given Jason to get rid of him had spoiled what might have happened with Brian.

What might have happened! Lord, what was she thinking? From the fire in that kiss, it was easy to imagine everything happening. She had plunged in over her head. She should be grateful he had put a stop to it.

Should be.

But she wasn't. Not for stopping it that soon, anyway.

She paced the room again. He was making her crazy. She had to do something, get him off her mind, plunge into something other than his arms.

She retrieved her shoes and sat to put them on. She would do a little late-night research. It was risky, but she was in the mood for some danger.

Several minutes later, when she walked into the first brightly lit saloon, she felt a tremor of doubt about the wisdom of her decision. The air was clouded with smoke and smelled of stale beer and sweat. Every soul in the saloon seemed to notice her the second she crossed the threshold, and all conversation came to an immediate stop.

"Evening, gentlemen," she said into the tense silence, hoping she sounded both confident and professional. "Would anyone here be willing to answer a few questions?"

In a moment she was surrounded by nearly everyone in the saloon, all shoving one another in an effort to get close to her, shouting their willingness to tell her anything she wanted to hear. Before she knew what was happening, a fistfight had broken out on the edge of the crowd, then another one.

One tall, lanky miner lifted her up and sat her on the bar. "Excuse me, ma'am," he said, tipping his hat. "Don't want you to get hurt. Don't you talk to no one till I get back." He waded into the melee and was lost from sight.

Alfie stared in horror at the destruction and violence taking place in front of her. Fists were swung indiscriminately, tables crashed under the weight of falling miners, chairs were wielded like clubs.

A shout and a pistol shot caught Alfie's attention and that of most of the men in the room. Several grunts and thuds indicated that a few combatants had gotten in one last lick before they'd stopped.

"What in the hell's going on here?" Marshal Hagman stood in the doorway, his recently fired pistol pointing threateningly at one miner after another. His eyes finally lit on Alfie where she sat on the bar. He nodded knowingly as he sauntered toward her. "If it ain't the lady reporter. You here arranging for some new bodies to study?"

Alfie decided to ignore the remark. "Marshal, I'm glad you arrived in time to stop the fight. I wanted to ask—"

"She's the one what started this, and she's gonna pay for everything that's broke."

Alfie turned to find the bartender, still safe behind the bar, glaring at her.

"I did not start this. I wanted to ask—"

Suddenly everyone in the room erupted in agreement with the bartender. "She started it."

"It was her, all right."

"Weren't no problem till she come in."

"Well, of all the . . . " Alfie considered trying to slide off the bar but decided that height, or altitude at least, gave her some advantage. She could actually look down on the marshal. "Of course I did not start the fight. It isn't my fault if these men are willing to use any excuse—"

"Run her in, Marshal."

"No, leave her to us. We'll take care of her."

Alfie couldn't tell who had spoken the last, but a chorus of laughter and general agreement followed it. Perhaps it would be best to leave.

"Tally up the loss, Jake," Hagman said, reaching over to grab Alfie's arm. "I'll lock her up till she pays."

Alfie slapped the hand away. "I can get down myself," she said. And she did make it to the floor, though about five hands reached out to steady her.

The tall miner who had lifted her up in the first place appeared at her side. "Pleasure to know you, ma'am." He reached up to tip his hat, discovered it was gone, and set off in search of it.

The marshal took her arm again and urged her softly, "Come on out of here while it's still easy."

She decided not to argue. As they reached the open doorway she heard the bartender shout, "Drinks on the little lady."

She tried to turn and protest but the marshal hustled her out the door.

"You're not really going to lock me up, are you?" At his incomprehensible grunt she added, "I do appreciate your coming in when you did. You handled that crowd very well." She gave a tug on her elbow but his fingers only tightened.

They had reached the jail and the marshal still hadn't spoken. "You know I didn't start that fight," she said.

He opened the office door and pushed her inside before he answered. "You didn't have no business being there. You was asking for trouble, and now you've got it."

A very young deputy came out of the back, rubbing his eyes sleepily. "What's goin'—" He jumped as if he had seen a ghost.

"Make Miss Foster comfortable in our best cell, Merle."

"Best cell?"

Hagman turned to Alfie. "I reckon the damages won't come to more than fifty dollars. A rich little woman like you—why, you can pay that now and I'll let you go on off to bed."

"All them cells is the same, Sheriff," Merle put in with a yawn.

Alfie tried to fight the sinking feeling in her stomach. "I don't have fifty dollars on me." She hoped her father had sent her the money she'd asked for.

"I'll walk you over to the hotel and—"

"I don't have fifty dollars with me. Listen, I can get it tomorrow. When the stage comes in—"

"Good. Then you won't be staying here but one night. Show her the city's hospitality, Merle."

"Hospa— what, sir?"

"Lock her up."

"Oh, yes, sir." Merle straightened his clothing and tried to look awake. Alfie almost laughed at his bleary-eyed expression, but she followed him through the door to the row of cells.

"You watch her close, Merle," Hagman hollered after them.

Alfie heard the outside door close.

"Whatcha done?" Merle asked, holding a cell door open for her.

Alfie walked inside, debating whether to answer him. It might be sort of fun to scare the fool boy, but it might be better to get him on her side. Besides, she had gone out for information, and it looked like Merle was the only one she had left to talk to. "Bring a chair, Merle," she said as he locked the door, "and I'll tell you all about it."

Chapter Eight

Alfie told her story with a few embellishments as the boy sat in an old chair outside her cell. He made no comment whatsoever, and she wondered if there was brain enough in his head to hold any information.

"Did you know the first two miners who were killed?" she asked after she had finished her story.

"Yes, ma'am."

She gave him a moment to elaborate, but he just stared at her sleepily. "Were they friends?"

The deputy wearily shook his head. "Near as I can tell, they didn't get on at all. Don't make no sense them bein' out there together."

"Maybe they weren't," Alfie mused. She had

assumed the killer had surprised them, but that didn't make sense, either. A knife wasn't like a gun, where a second victim could be killed before he recovered from the shock of seeing the first man killed. He should have had enough time to run. "Maybe the second victim stumbled on the scene after the first man was killed."

"No reason for them to be there separately, either," the deputy commented.

"Unless . . . " Alfie was pacing now, tapping her finger on her lip. "Maybe they had both gotten on somebody's wrong side. He lured them up on the mountain, killed them both as they arrived."

She made two more passes across the cell. "They were both surprised, though. The marshal said they were lying right together. Even if the second one didn't witness the first's death, he had to have seen the body. If he had bent over the body, he would have been stabbed in the back. Both men were stabbed through the heart. Why didn't the second man try to protect himself? There were no signs of bruising on either body. Maybe their dislike for each other would account for that."

She stopped to get the deputy's take on her speculations. He was sitting in an awkward position. "Deputy?" She watched him as, with a snore, he slowly toppled off his chair.

As he hit the floor, he came to for a brief

moment. He groaned and rearranged himself in a more comfortable position.

"Deputy? Could you answer a few more questions?"

The boy's response was a groan and another snore.

"Why don't you just sleep there?" she suggested. "I'd pass you a blanket but I don't have one either."

When he didn't respond, she decided he was taking her advice. She eyed the cot in the room, noting it was at least cleaner than the floor. She lay down but didn't expect to sleep. She ran several more possible scenarios through her mind before she drifted off.

The morning sun peeked through the window to hit Alfie square in the face. She rolled to a sitting position, yawned, and stretched. The cot hadn't been half-bad. The deputy, she discovered, was back in his chair, eyeing her with a mixture of suspicion and alarm.

"Don't you try nothin'," he said.

She stood and walked toward him. "Can I ask you a favor?"

"I ain't gonna let you out, no matter what you talk about," he warned. "I heard you're tricky."

She smiled as if he had told a clever joke. "When someone comes to relieve you, would you go over to the hotel and tell Mr. Brian Reed that I'm here?"

"Brian Reed. Yes, ma'am, I can do that. I'll tell him. Brian Reed." His lips moved over the name several more times as he memorized it.

Alfie stifled a groan. She hated to call this mishap to Brian's attention, but he was her best hope of getting out. If he wouldn't pay the damages, he could meet the stage and get the money her father was sending. The money she prayed her father would send.

The marshal could meet the stage as well, she knew, but he might decide to slip a few extra bills into his own pocket or increase the fine. She didn't trust any man who would lock a woman in a cell for no reason!

She was pacing the cell, her shoes tapping angrily on the stone floor, when someone yelled to Merle. "Back here," he responded.

"What kinda desperado you guarding?" Another young deputy came into view outside the cell. He watched Alfie for a moment, then turned to Merle. "She don't look too dangerous."

"No, sir," said Merle, "but she's tricky."

The newcomer nodded, a glint in his eye contradicting his otherwise serious demeanor. "I'll be careful. You go on now and get yourself some sleep."

He waited until the outside door slammed; then he took Merle's seat. "Merle's a little slow," he commented.

Alfie studied the new deputy. She would

probably be better off being pleasant, but a sharp retort would be so satisfying. "I notice you agree that I need careful watching."

"Naw," he said. "I doubt if you need it. You're just easier on the eyes than anything else around here."

His grin was almost charming. Or else Alfie needed more sleep. "Maybe you can tell me something about Mr. Wingate and his troubles at the mine."

He shook his head. "Don't really know much about it. He's sure had his trouble, though, ain't he? Say, you must be that lady reporter everybody's talking about. I heard you incited forty men to fight, and they done a thousand dollars worth of damage to the saloon."

Alfie scowled. "That whole building isn't worth a thousand dollars, even if you count the siding and the shingle nails."

The deputy shrugged. "It's what I heard, is all."

"I can see any information I get from you is going to be reliable." She turned back toward the cot. Maybe she should try to get some more rest. Besides, Brian might prove more sympathetic if she wasn't verbally dueling with the deputy when he came in.

Brian. Somehow, when she'd left his room after that tantalizing kiss, she hadn't envisioned their next meeting taking place with iron bars between them. He was such a strange man, and she wasn't sure what he thought of her, other than a flash of his desire that proved to be rather fleeting. Whatever his opinion, it wasn't likely to improve in the immediate future.

She stretched out on the cot and tried to rest. She had barely managed to relax when she heard the outside door open and close. She rolled to a sitting position, bracing herself for Brian's reaction. Instead the marshal joined the deputy outside her cell. They carried on a quiet conversation, which Alfie tried but failed to hear. With a nod in her direction, Hagman chuckled and left for the outer office. She wondered if they might have talked a little louder if she had pretended to be asleep.

Elbows on her knees and head in her hands, she calculated the length of time it would take Merle to get to the hotel, locate Brian, and explain the situation. Surely not this long. Merle had probably forgotten.

When the outside door opened again, she was on her feet before she even considered faking sleep. That soft voice in the outer office had to be Brian's. In a couple of minutes Brian and the marshal appeared outside her cell.

The marshal dismissed the deputy and turned to Brian. "Well?"

Brian nodded.

Hagman chuckled. "Told you it was her."

"Brian," she began. His face was completely

unreadable. But at least he had come. "I can explain."

"Reckon she can, boy," Hagman said. "She's one glib talker."

Alfie leveled her darkest scowl on him before returning her attention to Brian. "Brian, I need to borrow fifty dollars."

"Make that twenty-seven," Hagman put in. "There ain't no fine, just the damages. And one round of drinks."

Alfie knew her face registered her surprise. Brian reached for his wallet and counted out several bills. A moment later, Hagman opened the cell door.

"Thank you for your hospitality," Alfie said as she walked past the marshal.

"Anytime, miss," he said after her. "And I mean that quite literally. Stay out of the saloons or you'll be right back in here."

"Saloons?" Brian asked.

"Well, yes, I was in a saloon," she said irritably as they crossed the street. "I learned something, though."

"I would hope so."

She decided to ignore that. "The first two murdered men weren't friends."

Brian looked at her as if she had lost her mind.

"Think about it," she said. "Why would a man watch another be murdered and not worry that he would be the next victim? I think the second man killed was in on the first murder, then betrayed by his partner."

Alfie became aware of odd looks from a group of ladies who shared the boardwalk. Brian, she realized, was giving her the same odd look.

"Pursue any leads you want," he said. "I'm just after the ghost."

That didn't exactly reassure their fellow pedestrians. Alfie fought the urge to giggle.

"Something occurred to me as well," he went on, evidently oblivious to the stares. "Someone might have started the ghost rumors and even committed the murders for the sole purpose of closing down and hence devaluing the mine. We need to find out if someone's been trying to buy Wingate out."

They arrived at the door to the hotel, and he stopped her with a gentle hand on her arm. "Are you all right?"

Both the sudden question and the gesture startled her. "Why wouldn't I be?"

A trace of something unreadable flickered across his eyes. "I don't know. You just spent the night in jail after being involved in some sort of altercation. I just thought . . ."

Alfie blinked. The poor man wanted to be chivalrous and she wasn't giving him a chance. "You thought I'd need to cry on your shoulder for a few minutes?"

"You? Cry? I'm not that foolish." He quickly turned to open the door.

This time she was the one to stop him. "Brian, thank you for bailing me out of jail. I can pay you back as soon as the stage comes in this afternoon, I hope. Mostly, thanks for being concerned."

"I heard you go out."

He left the statement hanging, and she guessed the rest. "I'm not used to anyone worrying about me."

He nodded. "I'll try to remember that."

This quiet, serious conversation was almost as upsetting as last night's kiss. Alfie forced a smile and stepped toward the hotel. "Where's Katherine?"

He opened the door and let her pass. "When you didn't answer my knock, I left her in the care of the waiter. I was trying to convince the clerk to give me your key when the deputy found me."

Alfie pretended that none of that made her feel guilty. "Shall we join her?"

Brian escorted her into the dining room. She saw Katherine at once, sitting at a table staring sadly at a stack of pancakes, her doll held tightly on her lap. She looked up and squealed. In a moment she had clambered off her box and chair and thrown herself into Alfie's waiting arms.

Alfie let the girl cling to her for a full minute before she tried to pry her loose. "Your pancakes are getting cold," she said.

A telltale sniffle was her answer. Alfie stood with Katherine in her arms and carried her to the table. "It's all right now," she whispered.

She gave her one last squeeze before she sat her in her chair. Brian produced a handkerchief, and soon Katherine had pulled herself together.

"So," Alfie said brightly after she had ordered her own plate of pancakes. "What's on for today?"

"I'm going to talk to Wingate again," Brian said. "Try to find out if anyone's tried to buy the mine."

"I have some writing to do," Alfie said. "Katherine can stay with me while you're gone. Would you like that, sweetheart?"

Katherine nodded.

"Keep a close eye on her," Brian said.

Alfie turned to him, surprised that he didn't trust her with the child.

But Katherine had understood him better than she had. "I won't let her run away again, Daddy," she said.

After one last hug from Katie, Brian said goodbye to her and Alfie. When the door closed, he stood for a moment in the empty hall, sorting through his feelings. Alfie had missed his point earlier. He was the one who had wanted to cry on her shoulder, or at least to hold her so he knew she was all right.

When they hadn't gotten an answer at her door, Katie had been completely convinced that Alfie was dead. "Everybody dies," the girl had said sadly, and no assurances he could think of would sway her.

By the time he'd requested a key to her room, the child had nearly convinced him. In fact, when the deputy had come to tell him a young woman was in jail and asking for him, his first thought was that it was Katie's Aunt Candy in the cell. But it had been Alfie, and when he found her, she'd seemed completely unruffled. A barroom fight? So what? A night in jail? No problem. Scared little child? A bright smile will make it all right.

He started resolutely down the hall. Perhaps he was being unfair. Alfie hadn't known what he and Katie were going through while she was missing. And she hadn't asked them to worry about her. Besides, he had admired her independence, among other things, since he had first met her.

He rented a horse from the livery and rode the twisting track up to the mine office. Dale Wingate wasn't pleased to see him. At least not after he heard why Brian had come.

"What the hell difference does that make? All you need to do is find the ghost and perform whatever incantation will make it disappear, or prove there never was one. Just convince those lazy miners to come back to work. Otherwise, you stay the hell out of my business."

Brian spared a glance at the mine owner's son. The younger man didn't seem surprised by his father's outburst. Yet he made no move to calm him either.

"Mr. Wingate," Brian said, addressing the older man, "the ghost stories and the murders may be deliberate acts—ruses intended to reduce the value of your mine. I would like to question anyone who has made you an offer."

Wingate glared at him for a long moment. "Kline," he said finally. "Ted Kline. You want to know anything about him, you can ask the boy, here. They were thick as thieves a while back."

"Is that so?" Brian turned to the younger Wingate, trying not to picture him kissing Alfie at the bottom of the stairs.

"Take your conversation outside," Dale Wingate said. "I've got work to do."

Jason accepted his father's ill manners without comment. He made his way across the crowded office and opened the door, pausing to wait for Brian to join him. Outside he said, "Ignore the old man. I think sometimes he half believes there is a ghost."

"What makes you say that?" Brian asked, hoping he didn't sound as excited as he felt.

Jason grinned. "Things he says when he's in his cups. About Kline, the old man's right, we were friends when he first came to town. He had money and invested in several businesses, and most of them turned a healthy profit. He seemed to be a real mover. My father hates him because Kline talked him into investing in one of the businesses, probably the only one that failed. Maybe the old man's cursed."

Brian didn't return Jason's smile. "Why aren't you and Kline still friends? You don't seem to be easily influenced by your father's opinion."

Jason snorted. "He doesn't make it easy for me to agree with him on anything. No, Kline and I had our falling out because all the man cares about is money. We just decided to go our separate ways. I can't see him doing anything like this, though."

Brian nodded. "Thanks for the information." He walked to his horse, then turned back. "Do you play poker?"

"Some. You interested in a game?"

"I might be. You have an establishment of choice?"

Jason laughed. "I divide my evenings between the Gold Nugget and Molly's place."

"I assume your father drinks elsewhere."

"You hoping to hear the old man babble about a ghost?" He didn't wait for Brian's response. "He takes his drinks at the Jack of Diamonds. It pretends to be a little higher class than its neighbors."

With a quick wave, Brian mounted. As he descended the narrow path, he urged the horse to a gallop. He couldn't wait to get back and tell Alfie what he had learned.

"So now you think this Kline person invented the ghost and committed the murders so he could buy the mine," Alfie offered by way of summary.

Brian had entered her room a few minutes before and, after being enthusiastically greeted by Katherine, related his interview with the Wingates. He was in the chair opposite Alfie while Katherine sat on his lap, diligently working on the drawing she had started before his return.

"Not invented, exactly," he said. "Kline simply took advantage of an existing legend."

"So proving he committed the murders doesn't necessarily disprove the ghost story."

Brian hesitated a moment. "You have a point."

"Then why bother? I don't see how you're going to prove Kline committed the murders anyway. If you ask him he'll deny it. If he thinks you're on to him you could be corpse number four." She had said it lightly so as not to alarm Katherine, but she hoped Brian took her seriously. Asking questions about the ghost was one thing; going after a murder suspect was quite another.

Another thought brought a surge of warmth to her cheeks. If she was going to be examining his body, she wanted him alive. He was watching her with a rather curious expression on his face. Surely he couldn't have followed the same train of thought. She decided to change the subject.

"Are you really going to play poker with Jason?"

"No. Trebly told me he thought Jason cheated at cards. Besides, I'm a terrible poker player."

Alfie cocked her head to one side. "Now, that surprises me. I would have thought you had the perfect poker face."

"Oh, I can bluff," Brian said without the slightest change in his expression. "I'm just incredibly unlucky."

Katherine spoke without looking up from her furious sketching. "You can play poker with me."

Brian squeezed the girl. "Are you after my money?"

Katherine giggled. "I don't need your money. My turny says I'm rich."

Alfie and Brian eyed each other across the table. There it was again, "my turny." Alfie didn't have a clue. As for being rich, the number of dresses the little girl had was a fair clue as to her grandmother's wealth or at least her indulgence.

"Your grandmother called this man 'my turny'?" Brian asked.

"Yeah," Katherine said, brushing some hair out of her eyes with the back of her hand before she went back to her picture. "Like, 'My turny's coming today. You'll need to be quiet.' I usually just hid."

"My attorney?"

"Yeah," she said again, "my turny."

Alfie nodded. "I wonder how much he got

paid to put a little girl on a train by herself. We don't even know how long she was on that train before you met her in Kansas City."

"Not yet," Brian said softly, "but I have people working on it. Katie doesn't know where she's from."

"I can find Grandma's house from the park," Katherine supplied.

"And you can find this hotel room from any place in Glitter Creek," Brian said. Alfie caught a touch of pride in his voice.

Katherine pointed her pencil toward the ceiling. "Look for the tallest building. I can find it when Daddy's lost."

Alfie could imagine how Brian had made a game of the lesson. "Daddy gets lost a lot, does he?" she asked, trying but failing not to grin.

Katherine giggled. "He's not really lost. That would be scary!"

The smile Brian bestowed on the little girl was not one Alfie would have imagined possible of the preoccupied man she had met on the stage. He was more than fond of this child. He loved her. What was he going to do when he had to give her up?

"How's the picture coming?" he asked.

"It's mostly done," she said. "Here's you and me together and Alfie with the lantern. And this is the ghost. She's kinda floating here." She wiggled her hand over the drawing. "These are the trees and that's the moon so you know it's night."

"That's beautiful, Katie. I think we should frame it. Don't you think so, Alfie? It's an especially good likeness of you."

Alfie hadn't been paying much attention to the child's description. She had been watching Brian and worrying about the future. His future, not her own. She had to start reminding herself she wasn't to be part of his future, either.

Brian had turned the drawing and passed it across to her. The man and child were essentially stick figures, and the ghost was one long gown with a head. Katherine had drawn Alfie with an impossibly narrow waist, but otherwise quite well endowed.

She looked up and caught the glint in his eye. She quickly turned her attention to the little girl. "You've done a wonderful job," she said.

Katherine beamed.

Brian lifted her off his lap and stood. "I'd like to see if I can find Kline before noon. Can Katie stay with you a while longer?"

"Of course, but be careful."

"Don't worry. He'll never know why I'm questioning him."

Alfie wasn't convinced, but she let it go. "My job's easier than yours," she said just before he reached the door. "I don't have to prove anything."

"You mean you print unfounded rumors and unproven theories in your articles?" She knew his eyes well enough by now to know he wasn't as horrified as he pretended.

"Absolutely. I'm a good reporter."

"I've been warned you're a glib talker, too."

He left the room before she could respond. Katherine retrieved the picture to add some finishing touches. Alfie tried to bring her attention back to the article she had been writing.

It was hard to concentrate. She was worried about Brian. If Kline was the killer, and she hoped he wasn't, how could Brian question him without giving away his suspicions?

Brian was an intelligent, capable man. He also had a boyish innocence about him that was very appealing. And at this moment, terrifying.

She wanted to go with him. A reporter along might convey the notion that a story of the interview would expose the killer if something happened to Brian. Of course, that would put her in danger, too. Somehow that seemed less important, however, than Brian's safety.

She couldn't put Katherine in danger, too, though. And she wouldn't leave the little girl alone. She had been abandoned enough in her short life. If anything did happen to Brian, she resolved, she would take up the child's cause as her own, find a relative or a good home, or even keep her herself.

It would be almost like raising Brian's child.

She shook her head. Raising a child had never been part of any plan, dream, or fantasy.

And Katherine wasn't Brian's child. And Brian shouldn't be her concern at all.

Then why was she so worried?

Because they were friends. She had friends. Didn't she?

Actually she had been so caught up in her career and her dream of being a famous reporter that she had lost track of most of her friends. She competed with her fellow reporters. She argued with the Denver coppers. She ignored women and used men.

Brian was the closest friend that she had made in years.

And that was why she was so worried. Not because she was falling in love with him. She just couldn't be doing that.

"I wish I had paint so I could make the trees green and the moon yellow and our eyes blue. The ghost should be all shiny. What color makes shiny?" Katherine looked up from her picture and stared at Alfie. "Are you mad at me?"

"Oh, no, sweetheart," she said quickly, realizing she must have been scowling. "I'm just thinking about other things."

"Do you know how to make the ghost shiny?" the little girl persisted.

Alfie studied the picture, trying to concentrate. What the child had seen, of course, was the lantern in the trees when she had been left with Brian. She had only drawn them separately, Alfie and the ghost, because that was how she remembered what she hadn't understood.

"Maybe," Alfie said, "if you shade the pencil lightly over everything but the ghost and my lantern it will seem like they're shining."

"And the moon!" Katherine seemed delighted with the prospect. Alfie watched while she carefully did what Alfie had suggested. She waited until she was done to ask, "Have you ever used paints before?"

Katherine shook her head. "Grandma says they're too messy."

Alfie grinned. "I bet all you have to do is ask Daddy."

Katherine's answering grin seemed to reflect a new realization. Lord, she thought, what am I teaching this child? Proof, as if she needed it, that she was not cut out to be a mother.

Chapter Nine

Brian found Ted Kline in an office above one of the town's three banks. It was richly appointed with dark wood paneling and a polished oak desk. Kline himself seemed unusually well dressed. Either he was prospering, or he liked to appear as if he were.

"Are you looking to invest in this fine community?" Kline asked after Brian had introduced himself. He offered a box of cigars, taking one himself when Brian declined.

"No," Brian said, deciding that the town was small enough that a lie of that sort would be discovered rather quickly. Brian watched Kline's narrow eyes as he answered, "I've been hired by Dale Wingate to investigate the ghost rumors and the murders that have shut down his mine."

Brian was sure he detected a measure of discomfort. Whether it was from the general subject of the murders or something more personal was hard to tell.

"Odd that you should come to me, in that case," Kline said.

"Perhaps," Brian began, recalling Alfie's warning, "but Wingate will give me very little information about the mine itself, and, since I understand you made an offer for it, I thought you might have some pertinent information."

"Can't imagine what." He leaned back in his chair, seemingly at ease.

"The safety record at the mine, for instance," Brian said. "I thought perhaps you had checked into such things."

Kline shrugged. "Some odd little things have happened that were blamed on the ghost. Otherwise it was about like any other mine around. I've made offers for more than just Wingate's mine."

Brian nodded. "It's one of the oldest mines here. I'm surprised it isn't mined out."

Kline's smile looked almost genuine. "That just depends on if they've tapped all the veins."

Brian could feel the man's tension, though he tried to appear relaxed. There was a chance Kline was annoyed at having his day interrupted, but it could be something else. Brian had a feeling he would get to ask only a couple more questions.

"Does Winter's Gate have an untapped vein?" *How much do you want that mine?*

Kline's expression didn't change. "That's the hope, of course. Or perhaps I should say, that's the gamble."

Brian resisted the urge to hold his breath. "I'm sure Wingate's son, Jason, would have accurate information along those lines."

Kline didn't flinch. "I don't know how accurate his assessments would be. All he cares about is money."

Brian managed to nod blandly. "Thank you for your time, Mr. Kline." He rose to leave. Kline's head bent again over the papers on his desk. Before he turned away, Brian asked one last question. "Do you know anything about the feud between Jason and his father?"

Kline didn't look up. "I imagine they know each other too well."

Brian ran the conversation through his mind as he walked back to the hotel. He hadn't really learned anything. It was odd, though, that the former friends would each accuse the other of caring about nothing but money. What could it signify, other than the fact that they were probably both right?

It was easy to put Kline out of his mind as he approached the hotel. Alfie and Katie would be waiting for him. He hadn't realized how much more pleasant meals were when he shared them with interesting and beautiful companions.

"I'm having chicken," Katherine said. Her nose was pressed against the window glass as she watched the sidewalk below. "We hardly never had it 'cause Grandma said it was common, but Daddy says I can have whatever I want, so I'm gonna have chicken."

"That sounds good to me," Alfie said, hoping she was hiding her worry from the little girl.

She should have insisted on going with him. Katherine would have been perfectly safe, surely, and Alfie's presence would have served as a warning to Kline. Maybe. At the very least she would have known what was being said and how much danger Brian was creating for himself.

"Here he comes!" called Katherine. "Can we go down to meet him?"

It had been on the tip of Alfie's tongue to refuse. Brian would be at the door in a matter of minutes, anyway. Besides, he didn't need to know how worried she had been. But Katherine's eager expression changed her mind. She extended a hand toward the girl, and in a minute they were scurrying down the hall.

They reached the top of the stairs just as Brian entered the front door. Katherine slipped her hand out of Alfie's and scampered down the steps. Brian waited on one knee at the bottom and scooped her into his arms.

Alfie followed at a more sedate pace. Her worry for Brian took a different turn. These two were devoted to each other. Brian seemed to have no sense of self-preservation at all. What would he do when he lost her?

"Are you ready to eat?" he asked her over the top of Katie's little blond head.

Alfie nodded her assent as Katherine answered. "You have to come see my picture first."

"I saw your picture," Brian said, setting her back on her feet.

"But I finished it. Let me show you."

"Besides, I didn't lock the door," Alfie said, moving to follow the girl up the stairs.

Brian's hand on her arm slowed her pace. "Were you that eager to see me?" he asked softly.

"Katherine was," Alfie answered lightly, then paused, bringing Brian to a stop. Katherine had made it to the top of the stairs and was hurrying down the hall. "What are you going to do when you have to give her up?"

The eyes that met hers were surprisingly revealing.

"Maybe I won't," he answered after a moment.

"Brian," she admonished, "you can't just keep a child."

Brian glanced toward the top of the stairs. Katherine was out of sight, but they both knew she was waiting. "My guess is that Candace is her last living relative, or her grandmother's attorney wouldn't have sent her this far. Once that's settled for sure, I'll adopt her."

"Do you think they'll let a single man adopt a little girl?" She hated to make it sound so unnatural, but that was the way a judge would probably see it.

"Then I'll get married."

He started up the stairs and Alfie hurried after him. "Just like that?" It was more an accusation than a question.

"Are you applying?" he asked.

"Don't be ridiculous."

Katherine appeared at the top of the stairs or she might have said more, although she wasn't sure what. She couldn't very well point out that he wouldn't know how to take care of a child, since he seemed to be doing just fine. And how was she going to explain the knot in her stomach when he suggested finding a wife?

While Brian and Katherine went into the room, Alfie chose to remain in the hall. The more she thought about what Brian had said, the more upset she became. She had been trying to warn him, to protect him. He'd not only refused to heed her advice, but he'd made light of it with a silly suggestion.

She held her tongue when the two stepped back into the hall. Brian had picked up her reticule and handed it to her. She fished out the room key and moved to lock the door. She would have liked weighty silence while she listened for the click, but Brian asked Katherine if she wanted to bring her doll, to which Katherine replied that her doll couldn't eat fried chicken. This led to a lively discussion about how much chicken the two of them could consume.

Alfie turned finally, dropping the key back into her bag. At least they had waited for her, she thought sourly, then wondered where that thought had come from. Was she feeling left out? Was she envious of what Brian had with the little girl? Surely not. Not when she knew it couldn't last and would only leave heartbreak behind.

Well, *she* wasn't falling into that trap, she told herself as she watched Katherine slide down the banister with Brian's careful assistance. She would leave Glitter Creek with no more entanglements than she'd had when she'd come. Her heart wasn't going to be broken by a little girl, and certainly not by a man. Oddly enough, the observation didn't make her feel better.

She felt Brian's eyes on her as she descended the last few steps and joined the pair at the bottom. She had to force herself to meet his gaze, afraid some of her turmoil would show on her face. No, she was afraid he'd see the longing she hadn't acknowledged until that moment.

He was silent as he escorted her and Katherine to the dining room. Katherine skipped away toward the corner, where the waiter kept the box she always sat upon.

Brian's hand stopped Alfie from following. "You're right, of course," he said softly. "I could easily lose her. But I might not, and she's worth risking everything for."

Alfie thought he had more to add to the admission, but Katherine had picked out a table and was struggling to get the box situated on a chair. In moments Brian had helped her up and held a chair for Alfie.

She cursed herself for not being quick enough to slip into the seat while he was helping Katherine. She had lingered behind, hoping some distance between them would help clear her mind. Now she was to be in close proximity to him again, to allow him to help her, to experience, perhaps, his accidental touch. And pretend it didn't make her heart race.

The question in his eyes let her know he had sensed her reluctance. She slid quickly into the chair as he helped her position it. She was glad, she really was, that it was over in seconds and he had taken his place between her and Katherine.

Brian let Katherine order her chicken and asked for the same. Alfie went along to avoid making a decision. Why was she suddenly feeling so confused? It was as if Brian had told her something shocking, something she hadn't previously known. But he really hadn't.

She knew he was checking into Katherine's family. She had guessed he wanted to keep her.

Hadn't she vowed only minutes ago to raise the child as her own if something happened to Brian?

No. She had vowed to find her home; raising her had been an afterthought, a scenario of last resort.

She deliberately yanked herself back to the present, to the table, to the presence of Brian and Katherine. "What did you learn from Kline?" she asked, proud that her voice sounded normal.

Brian laughed. "Welcome back."

Katherine spoke before she could respond. "She was a million miles away."

"I'm sorry," Alfie said, smiling at Katherine before she turned toward Brian. "I was working on an article when we saw you coming. I guess my mind's still with it."

It was a wonderful excuse. It tripped easily off her tongue, and, while it wasn't true, strictly speaking, it had been the case often enough that she didn't even feel dishonest.

Or she didn't until she saw Brian's face. He nodded his understanding, but his eyes watched her speculatively.

"I didn't learn much from Kline," he said after a moment, "other than a few impressions."

She couldn't resist asking, "What did he learn from you?"

"That I don't smoke," he answered lightly. At her scowl, he added softly, "Are you worried about me?"

Alfie glanced at Katherine. She seemed to be engrossed in tracing the pattern on the tablecloth with the handle of her spoon. "Yes," she fairly hissed at him. "You can chase your ghost all you want, but these murders are another matter. You're out of your depth."

He nodded as if considering some sage advice. "I'm sure you're right," he said, "but that doesn't explain why *you're* worried."

She felt trapped. He knew she cared about him. He was trying to force her to admit it. She wanted to smack that thoughtful look right off his face. "It would be such a nuisance," she said, "having to write about one more murder."

He actually grinned at her.

Alfie waited at her door as Brian and Katherine walked the short distance to theirs. "Have a good nap," she said, grinning at Brian. Katherine had promised to be quiet all afternoon so he could sleep. The little girl would never admit to needing a nap herself. She took the key Brian handed her and, with her tongue between her teeth, tried to fit it in the keyhole.

Brian didn't return Alfie's smile. "You're not leaving on the stage, are you?" he asked.

She shook her head. "I'm sending a story, but I'm sticking around. Remember, I owe you some money."

He smiled then, barely. "Could Katherine stay with you this evening? I'd like to talk to Wingate in a more . . . congenial setting."

"That's fine," she said.

Katherine managed to get the key to fit in the lock and opened the door to Brian's room. He gave her a much bigger smile and followed her in, with one last glance at Alfie.

Alfie shook her head. He was, she reminded herself, the strangest man she had ever met. She grabbed the doorknob with one hand to steady it as she inserted the key, and felt the door move inward.

She stood for a moment gazing at it. She knew she had locked the door, or tried to. She had been so agitated she must not have gotten it locked. Her heart was pounding just the same as she pushed the door open.

Nothing looked disturbed. The bed, her clothes, seemed just as she had left them. She stepped cautiously into the room, breathing a sigh of relief when she knew for certain that no one waited for her inside.

Her relief was followed immediately by concern. There was the definite smell of smoke in the air. She had detected cigar smoke on Brian's clothes when he had come from Kline's office. Had Kline been in her room?

She hurried to the table, where her half-finished article lay amid scattered notes. A quick survey told her nothing was missing, though whether anything had been disturbed was hard to tell.

After a moment, she wanted to laugh at herself. Of course nothing had been disturbed.

Who would be searching through her room? The smoke she smelled had been brought in by Brian himself. She had been too rattled to get the door locked properly, that was all.

She turned and closed the door, dropping her reticule on the bed. In a few minutes she was engrossed in her writing. It was so much easier to work, she thought, without distractions. Katherine's presence, she realized, hadn't really bothered her. Brian's absence had. Knowing he was safely sleeping in the next room did wonders for her concentration.

Just after dark Brian made his way toward San Francisco Street. Discordant music and laughter greeted him as he came down the narrow steps. He was conscious of leaving a more pleasant, though perhaps less exciting, world behind.

After a short walk he found the entrance to the Jack of Diamonds. Unlike the other saloons with their swinging doors, this establishment had large oak doors that seemed incongruous with the rest of the clapboard construction. His guess was that they had been brought in at great expense from Denver to lend an elegant air to the place.

Inside, though the air was just as smoky and the music just as loud as in the other saloons he had seen in this town. The appointments were a little nicer, perhaps.

And this time Brian was greeted by what he

assumed to be the bouncer. Brian was expecting to be asked for a cover charge or given some warning about proper behavior. Instead the man looked him over, then stepped out of his way.

Brian glanced back at the bouncer as he stepped farther into the room. The man was keeping the peace through intimidation, he assumed.

At the bar he turned, leaned his elbows behind him, and studied the room. He found Wingate at a far table with a couple of other men. As he watched, one of the men got up and moved on to other friends.

"What can I get for you?" a voice behind him asked.

Brian looked over his shoulder. He considered buying a bottle to ply Wingate with, but decided from the looks of things that the man was already drinking heavily. He hated to encourage him to drink more.

He shook his head and turned back to watch his quarry. Would the man's other companion leave as had the first? Would someone else join him before that happened? Perhaps it wasn't wise to wait too long.

Brian walked to Wingate's table. "Is this a private conversation, or might I join you?"

"Sit down, boy," invited Wingate. "Nick, this is the boy I told you about. Says he can find my ghost."

Nick laughed but stretched a hand toward

him. "Nick Glover. I own the mine around the mountain from Dale's. One of these days our tunnels are going to bump up against each other in that poor old mountain."

"When that happens," Wingate said, "I'll have to figure the gold's all gone."

Brian didn't let them see his reaction. These men seemed to be good friends, but from what they had just said, Glover could gain a great deal from Wingate's mine being closed. "Have you seen the ghost, Mr. Glover?" he asked.

"Nope," he answered cheerfully. "And this is my last drink." He refilled his glass from the bottle at the table and passed it back to Wingate.

"Ain't you drinking, boy?" asked Wingate.

Brian shook his head. "Altitude," he said, hoping that would suffice as an excuse.

Wingate snorted.

Glover downed the drink and rose from the table. "Take it easy, Dale," he said. "Nice to meet you . . ."

"Reed. Brian Reed," he supplied.

"Reed, if you manage to scare off that ghost of Dale's, try not to send it toward my mine, all right?"

Brian smiled. "I'll be careful."

Wingate snorted again.

When Glover was gone, Brian turned to a less friendly Wingate. "Nice fellow. Known him long?"

Wingate nodded and refilled his glass.

It hadn't occurred to Brian that he might have difficulty broaching the subject. How many drinks would it take for Wingate to admit he'd seen the ghost? Surely not too many more.

"I heard a rumor, Mr. Wingate," he began. "I'm sure you've heard it, too."

"This about the ghost?"

"Yes, sir."

Wingate pushed his glass aside and heaved a sigh. "You've come to ask me if I know they like to say the ghost is my wife."

"Some folks say she died under mysterious circumstances."

"Nothing mysterious about it," Wingate said. "Was the fault of the boy."

Brian hid his surprise. "Jason?"

"Yeah. The boy was about twelve. Causing trouble. We lived in a little house right near our mine, back then. Worked it by myself till I hit the lode. Anyhow, the boy had done something wrong, can't remember what. Patsy went looking for him. He was hiding out, not wanting to be found. She fell down a test hole. Broke her neck."

Brian closed his eyes. That explained the rift between father and son. "Have you seen her?" he asked softly.

Wingate snorted. "I'm not ignorant like these superstitious fools. I don't believe in ghosts." He paused. "No offense."

"None taken," Brian said mildly.

"Can't you go up there and put on some show or other and then announce that the ghost is gone? I'm tired of waiting."

"Sir, I'm not convinced that the ghost, whether she exists or not, is the real cause of your problems. Somebody killed three men on that mountain."

"Their grievances got nothing to do with my mine." Wingate disconsolately poured another drink, ignoring Brian.

Brian watched him for a few minutes, then decided not to wait to see if he'd admit to seeing the ghost. It wouldn't really matter anyway. He rose and left the table, uncertain whether Wingate had even noticed his departure.

Outside, he sat down on a bench in front of the building. What evidence did he really have? A father who had never forgiven his son for his wife's death. A former friend of that son who wanted to buy the father's mine. Two dead men who might have been part of a plot to shut down the mine. Another who saw the ghost regularly. He had no idea how to solve the murders.

And the ghost? Damn, he'd like to see her. He paused. There was nothing to stop him from going up the mountain where Trebly had died and waiting until dawn.

He rose and headed toward the stairs that led to Main Street. Halfway there two men came out of a saloon right in front of him. Having nearly collided with them, Brian excused himself and was about to move on when one of them stopped him.

"Say, ain't you the guy we've heard about come to get rid of the ghost?"

Brian studied the man in the light from the window. He looked to be middle-aged, sober, and not particularly threatening. "Yes, that's me. Have you seen her?"

The man exchanged a glance with his companion before he answered. "Not exactly. But we both seen what it done. Lot of tricks in the mine, some of 'em dangerous, though nobody got hurt, 'cept Perkins and James."

"We're gettin' a little shy on money," his companion said, "and were wondering if it's safe to go back to work yet."

"I don't think so," Brian said, knowing his employer wouldn't like to hear him say it.

"We tried other mines," the first put in, "but one folded, and the other weren't safe. 'Sides, Wingate paid better."

"I'm sorry," Brian said. "I think somebody wants that mine closed. If you and the others go back to work, those tricks you mentioned might become more serious."

He was about to ask more about the tricks and if Perkins and James might have had anything to do with them, when they heard the report of a pistol. The bullet imbedded itself in the wood of the building behind them.

Brian and his companions dove for the ground. The small pocket pistol Brian carried in the lining of his coat was in his hand before he hit the dirt.

"What the hell?" yelled one of the men.

"Are you hurt?" called his friend.

"Naw, I'm fine, if being shot at qualifies."

They had all managed to land outside the pool of light from the window. A few people came out of the saloons to investigate.

Certain that whoever had shot at them was long gone, Brian came to his feet, returning his pistol to its pocket. The men he had been talking to eyed him from some distance away, as if afraid that being near him might invite another shot.

"Did anybody see where the shot came from?" he asked.

The gathering crowd murmured, but no one offered any information. "Of course not," he muttered, brushing the dirt from his pants and coat. In the process he discovered a neat little hole right through his coattail. He stuck his finger in the hole and grinned. He must be stepping on the right person's toes. Now, whose were they?

After being shot at, it seemed foolish to go hiking around on the mountain alone. The ghost would have to make her predawn walk without him.

Brian studied the buildings across the street, certain that the shot had come from one of them or the alleys in between. It was interesting, he thought, to discover that Molly's place was one of those buildings. He walked back into the window's light and tried to stand where he had been. He found the bullet in the base of the siding, lined it up with where he had stood, and gazed again across the street. Upstairs. The shot had been fired through an upstairs window.

The crowd had become quiet, watching him. He was only half-aware of them. "Interesting," he muttered. Interesting also was the fact that no one from that establishment had come out to investigate the shot. Perhaps it had been because, when the occupants had heard it, they'd rushed upstairs instead of outside.

He walked purposefully across the street and up onto Molly's porch. He knocked on the door. Only then was he aware of the encouraging shouts from the men behind him. From the sound of it, they thought he was going there to celebrate the fact that he had just survived being shot at.

An impassive Rusty answered the door as he had before, then stepped back to allow him entrance. "Are you here to see anyone in particular?"

"I need to speak to Molly."

"Molly's busy. You can wait in the parlor with the others."

Piano music and feminine laughter emanated from that direction, along with the scent of smoke and perfume.

"Does she have an office where I can wait?"

Scowling, Rusty directed Brian to a homey little dining room. After getting his name, he promised to let Molly know he was there.

Brian walked around the room, looking at the odd assortment of bric-a-brac. He didn't have to wait long. Molly breezed into the room, smiling brightly. "Well, if it isn't the nice young man who brought Candy's niece by. How is the little darling? Did you find her a home?" She joined him by the cold fireplace.

"She's in good hands," Brian said.

"I'm so glad to hear it. Did you want to talk to Candy?"

"No. I thought you might be able to help me. Was a gun fired upstairs a few minutes ago?"

Molly seemed taken aback. "Why, yes. Harmless little accident. It happens sometimes when the customers have had too much to drink. Why?"

Brian stuck his finger in the hole in his coat and held it up for her to see. "I don't think it was an accident."

She gave him a blank stare.

"I was across the street," Brian said by way of explanation.

"But I'm sure it was an accident. I don't think he even knew the bullet went out the window."

"And who would he be?"

"Look," she said, turning to steel, "I won't be responsible for any violence. If you want to report this to the marshal, and if the marshal comes around and asks, I'll give him the name." She turned to leave.

"Ma'am." He was surprised she stopped. "Do I look like I want to call the man out?" He held his coat open so she could see the absence of guns on his hips. "If somebody's trying to kill me, I need to know about it."

She studied him a moment, then came forward. "He said it was an accident. He dropped his gun belt, and the gun discharged. Candy said so, too."

"Candy?"

"Why, yes. He's upstairs with Candy."

"Who?" Brian took a step toward her, his eyes probing hers. "I need his name."

She was silent for only a moment. "Jason," she said, "Jason Wingate."

Chapter Ten

Alfie scrambled for the door when she heard the knock. She had gone to bed early, unable to remember when she had last had a full night's sleep. She had no idea if it was midnight or early morning, but she knew the knock was Brian's.

He nearly burst into the room. "I think we're on the right track," he whispered excitedly, drawing her farther into the room.

"What?"

He moved quickly to the window and glanced out. She followed him, but he pulled her into the corner. "Stay away from the window," he whispered.

She was very close to him, his hands on her

arms keeping her there. She should have been uncomfortable with his manner, with his closeness, with the heat of his hands soaking through the thin fabric of her robe. She was actually comfortable enough to lean toward him—so he could hear her, of course. "What's going on?"

"Kline and Jason Wingate are partners. They're in some scam to get the mine from Jason's father. I think Perkins and James were working for them, playing dirty tricks in the mine to scare away the miners."

"How do you know this?" He had actually brought in some rather chilly air. It was odd that she felt so warm.

"Look." He bent his head and raised a corner of his coat.

Alfie was momentarily distracted by the fact that his hair would be so easy to run her fingers through. She caught herself and looked down to make out what he was showing her. "There's a hole in your coat," she whispered. "So?"

He smiled, obviously pleased. "Jason shot at me."

"Jas—"

She had forgotten to whisper, and he clapped a hand over her mouth. With a nearly silent chuckle he eased his hand away. It felt like a caress. She stared at him a moment, then tried again. "Jason shot at you?"

He nodded.

"And you're pleased. You enjoyed it?"

"No." He laughed. "But that proves we're on to something. We're getting close and he's getting scared."

"He's getting scared?"

Brian nodded enthusiastically.

"You're crazy."

He just grinned.

"Look, this doesn't make any sense. If Jason is a cold-blooded murderer, why didn't he just kill his father?"

"I don't know. Maybe someone else will inherit the mine. I wouldn't put it past the old man. He blames his son for his wife's death."

She stared at him, trying to read his eyes in the dark. She felt her heart race and wondered if it was out of fear for him or desire. Being this close was doing odd things to her insides. After a moment she whispered, "You should go."

"I can't just run away. I need to tell my suspicions to Wingate. We might be able to expose Jason. If the man's a murderer—"

"No." She heard her voice tremble. "I mean . . . you should go. Leave my room."

He was still for a moment, and she thought he might not have understood. Finally, he drew her closer. "I'm not running from you, either."

His lips descended slowly to meet hers. The effect was tantalizing. Her tongue reached out to taste him before she remembered his earlier reaction to her boldness. She hesitated, only to find his lips parting in encouragement.

Her fingers were already splayed across his shirtfront, she wasn't sure since when. They trailed down his ribs and around to his back, pulling his body closer while her tongue played with his.

Desire, which had begun with his first touch, burst into full bloom, sending her beyond reason. His hands on her backside reminded her of just how little she was wearing. Instead of making her feel ashamed, however, the knowledge made her more excited. She willingly, wantonly, let him lift her and press her tightly against his hardened body.

She heard him groan as he wrenched his lips from hers. She whimpered in protest but found his neck accessible, and happily turned her attention there. She nipped and sucked, proudly eliciting another groan from deep in his throat.

"Katie," he whispered.

Shock brought her back to her senses, or partially. He was thinking about another woman! As she began to draw away, she realized he was talking about the little girl.

He didn't let her leave his arms. "I'm sorry," he said near her ear, panting. "I don't want to stop any more than you do, but . . . " He struggled to catch his breath, then, with a curse, collapsed against the wall, bringing her with him. "That was one hell of a kiss. But I knew to expect that."

She was panting, too, leaning against his

chest. "How do parents . . . ?" No, that question was way too forward.

He chuckled. "Parents normally have more than one room."

She shouldn't say it. She would. "So do we."

He sighed, caressing her cheek. He ran his fingers through her hair, trailing down the length of it. "Let's not get swept away by the heat of the moment. If you let me love you, I don't want any regrets."

She turned to look up at him, surprised that she could grin. "Do you think you'd regret it?"

He nodded somberly. "If you hated me afterward, I'd regret it. Alfie, I want to make love to you, but I need more than just that. I can't risk losing you."

She rested her head against his chest again. Her breathing was still labored and she could feel his heart pounding under her ear. "You're so noble I want to slap you," she said.

He chuckled. "Not a bad idea, under the circumstances."

With one last hug, he set her upright and moved away from the wall. Away from her. "I'd better go," he said. "Shall I take Katie?"

"No," Alfie whispered. "Let her sleep."

He started toward the door, then came back, placing a quick kiss on her cheek. "Good night."

In a moment he was gone. Alfie stood staring at the door. He was right, of course. They had no future together. She wasn't a wanton, though her behavior probably had him thinking as much. He was the only man who'd ever made her behave this way. Still, she wished he'd come back.

Even as she wished it, the door opened. Brian stuck his head into her room. She was about to run to him when he whispered, "Lock this door," and was gone.

Alfie groaned in exasperation but did as he said. With the door locked, she crawled back into bed beside Katie, wondering how long it would take for the frustration to subside enough for her to sleep.

Brian and Katie had just made their usual swift descent to the bottom of the stairs the next morning when Helen, the woman who had checked him in, approached them. She frowned down at Katie but said nothing about their use of the banister.

"This message was brought to me earlier by one of the men from Glover's mine." She handed him the note and marched back to her place behind the desk.

Alfie joined him as he opened the note. "What is it? From Glover?"

"No," he said, scanning it quickly. "It's from Wingate. He must have caught the miners coming in off shift. He wants to see me."

"Now?" asked Katie. "But I'm hungry."

"Of course not now. He can wait until my assistant's had her breakfast. Can't have your tummy rumbling while we're trying to talk." He tickled her for emphasis and she giggled.

They found a table in the dining room and placed their orders. Brian watched Alfie sip her coffee. She was very quiet this morning, probably regretting last night's kiss. All the more reason for him to have stopped it when he did.

"What are you up to today?" he asked, hoping it sounded casual.

She set her cup down and folded her arms on the edge of the table. "There's not much new I can add to yesterday's installment on the murders. I might interview the marshal again, see if he has any hope of solving the crimes. After that I don't know."

He watched her steady gaze, fearing to give voice to his suspicion. "Are you thinking about leaving?"

Her eyes flicked away from his. "I don't know. I have to keep working. There doesn't seem to be anything here." He thought he heard a wistfulness in her voice, but maybe it was only his imagination.

"You could write a story about the little orphan who came west to find a home."

He thought a smile touched the corners of her lips. "Wrote it."

He nodded. Of course she had. "How about your story on the investigator hunting for ghosts?"

She looked mildly uncomfortable. He guessed she'd written that one, too. "You could write a second installment," he suggested. "He got shot at last night."

"Who did?" Katie interrupted.

Brian smiled at the girl. "Just somebody on the street. Nobody was hurt." This seemed to satisfy her, and she went back to lining up her silverware.

Brian turned back to Alfie, raising his brows. "I could give you the details."

She was quiet. He was afraid she wasn't considering what he said as much as she was considering how to tell him she was leaving. He gave it another try. "Besides, you don't know how any of these stories are going to end. Stay a little longer. At least don't make a decision until we hear what Wingate wants."

After a moment she leaned toward him, speaking very softly. "Brian, there's a possibility that Kline was in my room while we were having dinner last night. If he was, he read my article, the one where I suggest a local businessman could be trying to devalue the mine so he could buy it more cheaply. That could be the reason you were shot at. I feel as if I've put you in danger."

"Kline was in your room?"

"I don't know," she said. "The door was unlocked and I could smell cigar smoke."

"But if that's so, it lends more credence to my theory, since it was Jason who shot at me." This last he managed to whisper so as not to alarm

Katie. She happily played a game of hopscotch with her silverware. "Besides," he whispered fiercely, "I'm sure the shot was intended to scare me off."

"Maybe you should let it," she whispered just as fiercely.

Brian sat back and watched her sip her coffee. Her hands trembled ever so slightly. From fear? Anger? He couldn't read her mood this morning, which was odd. He was usually pretty good at that.

Perhaps, he thought, her mood had nothing to do with shots fired or articles written. Perhaps she was scared of her own reaction to last night's kiss. He had to fight to keep a smile off his lips, a smile he was certain would appear rather arrogant.

"Are you running from *me?*" he whispered.

She looked startled, ready to argue, but the waiter arrived with their plates, giving her an excuse to ignore him. In fact, she managed to ignore him through most of the meal.

"Katherine had better stay with me," she said as they were finishing.

"She can come, if she wants to," Brian said.

"Are you sure that's safe?" she asked softly.

"I'm just taking a buggy up to Winter's Gate. She's been up there before."

"But," she argued, nearly whispering, "this could be a trap."

Brian went still. He hadn't thought of that.

"You're right," he said softly. "She'd better stay with you. I can get up and back faster on horseback, anyway."

After settling Katie and her doll in Alfie's room, he rented a horse and rode to Winter's Gate. Wingate answered his knock with a growled command to enter.

Inside, Wingate sat behind his desk, and, as usual, his son was present, lounging in a chair at the far end of the little office. "You wanted to see me?" Brian asked, forcing himself to ignore the younger Wingate.

"Yeah," said the old man. "You're fired."

"I beg your pardon?" How he would love a chance to talk to him without his son present. He knew that was very unlikely.

"Here's what I figure I owe you," Wingate said, handing him a cashier's check.

"Mr. Wingate," Brian began, "please reconsider—"

"Too late. I've sold the mine to Ted Kline. Let him battle the damn ghost. I'm goin' down to Denver to that house I built four years ago before I'm too damn old to enjoy it. Shoulda done it months ago. The boy here can work for Kline or find his own strike. Ain't none of it my worry anymore."

Brian risked a glance at Jason. He seemed unmoved by the conversation. Of course, this was undoubtedly old news to him. Brian saw no alternative but to take the money and go. He turned at the door and addressed the elder Wingate. "I'm sorry I couldn't help you."

Wingate waved him away.

On the way back to town he considered what he should do. He didn't want to leave until he had tried again to see the ghost. That particular activity was probably no safer now than it would have been the night before. In fact, if his theory was correct, Jason was going to look with considerable suspicion on him if he didn't leave town immediately.

But he didn't want to do that. If he was going to be honest with himself, which he normally was, his desire to stay had nothing to do with the ghost.

Still an interesting thought occurred to him just as the town of Glitter Creek came into clear view below him. If Alfie had decided to leave town, he was free to do so as well. He could stay in Denver, where the telegraph service would put him in easy communication with his associates. He could pursue legal adoption of Katie from the territorial capital.

The more he thought about it, the more he liked the plan. He had it ready to present to Alfie when he knocked on her hotel door. To his surprise, Alfie opened the door and threw her arms around his neck, sobbing. "I'm so sorry! So sorry!"

"Alfie, what is it?" He had to nearly lift her in

order to enter the room and close the door. He led her to the bed and set her down beside him. "Hush now; tell me what's wrong."

But even as he asked it, he knew. Katie was gone.

A cold knot formed in the pit of his stomach and he waited, frozen, for Alfie to tell the story.

"A woman came and got her," Alfie said, her words broken by sobs. "Her Aunt Candy. She had a letter from a lawyer she said proved the girl was hers. She brought the marshal with her. I didn't know what to do. I should have done something."

She gave in completely to her tears, and Brian pulled her against him, rocking her gently as she cried. "There was nothing to be done," he said to soothe her. But even as he said it he was hoping it wasn't true.

Alfie's tears were soon spent, and he dried them with a clean handkerchief. "Better?" he asked.

"Oh, Brian," she said with a moan.

"Hush, now," he murmured, afraid she was going to cry again. "Did you see the letter?"

She took a deep, shuddering breath and seemed in control again. "I saw it briefly. It was from the grandmother's attorney. I think it was intended to arrive before Katherine. It mentions money that is held in trust for Katherine that Candy will control."

"And that's why she wants her," Brian said. "We won't let her keep her."

"What are we going to do?"

Brian stood and paced across the room. He considered and dismissed kidnapping. He'd rather have the girl legally. That, however, could take some time. "When the stage comes in the afternoon, I'll ask the driver to send a telegram for me when he gets back to Denver. Meanwhile, I'm going to go visit Katie, make sure she's all right. Maybe I can talk some sense into Candy."

Alfie shook her head. "I think she wants that money too much."

"She can have the money," Brian said, knowing his voice was harsher than he intended. "All I want is the little girl."

"Brian," she began, then paused, as if uncertain whether she should say what was on her mind.

Brian took a deep breath, trying for calm. "What?"

"With that money she might be able to leave her profession and start a new life. She might make a good home for Katherine."

Brian gave that thought the span of two heartbeats to soak in before he turned and left the room. He all but ran down the stairs, trying not to acknowledge any truth in what Alfie had said. But of course, he had no choice, and that was why it made him so furious. He didn't want to believe anyone else could be as good for the child as he.

Outside, he hurried across the street, ignoring the curses of horsemen and drivers, and ran down the steps to San Francisco Street. In a moment he was at the door to Molly's house.

Alfie was tempted to cry all over again. Why couldn't she have kept her mouth shut? She didn't even get a chance to ask him how she might help. Perhaps her father's attorney could offer some legal advice. She would get a letter off to him on today's stage. Meanwhile, she would carry out the only plan that had occurred to her while she waited for Brian.

She changed into the green dress she had worn on her date with Jason, and pinned up her hair in as fashionable a chignon as she could manage. She locked and tested her door on her way out and walked slowly toward the marshal's office, her mind racing through several possible openings.

Marshal Hagman was in, his feet propped on his desk while he visited with Merle, the young deputy. He gave her a slow once-over as he brought his feet to the floor. "My, my. The feisty little lady's sure dressed to kill, wouldn't you say, boy?"

The deputy eyed her with wonder and fear. "She's tricky, sir."

Alfie tried for a humble smile, ignoring the deputy. "I came to apologize."

"Now, ain't that nice. Deputy, why don't you find something else to do?"

"Like what, sir?"

"I don't know. Just get the hell outta here."

"Oh. Yes, sir." The boy started for the door. "I'll come back and check on you after a while."

"You do that." He leered at Alfie. "Now, about that apology?"

Alfie gritted her teeth and plunged ahead. "I said some nasty things to you when you came for the girl—"

"You cast doubt on my mother's virtue," he commented, slouching lazily in his chair.

"Yes, well, I was upset." She strolled around his office, having difficulty bringing herself to approach the marshal. "You see," she said, spinning around to face him, glad that the whole room separated them, glad that he hadn't left his chair, "that little girl has come to mean a lot to me . . . and my friend, and I guess I lost my head."

"Your temper is what you lost," he said.

"Well, yes, that's true. But now I've come to ask you a favor."

"Uh-huh. So you didn't really come to apologize."

She had already apologized! Alfie wanted to scream at him. But that would probably be counterproductive. "I came for both," she said a little too sweetly.

Hagman laughed. "Tell me the favor, and we'll get back to the apology."

Alfie felt a surge of fury and tamped it down. She really disliked this man. "All right," she managed, approaching the desk. "I would like you to sign a paper saying that you, as an officer of the law, are aware of how Candace Dreher makes her living, and, that unless she shows immediate signs of amending her ways, she's not fit to raise Katherine Abbott."

Hagman looked at her for a long time. She felt heat rising to her face as she struggled to control her temper. Finally he spoke. "Do you really think that'll do any good?"

"I don't know!" she blurted. "It can't hurt, and I have to do something."

He chuckled and pulled a wanted poster from his desk and flipped it over. As he wrote on the blank side, he read aloud. "As marshal of this here town of Glitter Creek, I know for a fact that Candy Dreher is a soiled dove, and not a par-tic-u-ler good one at that. She also drinks like a fish, consorts with lowlifes, and swears like a sailor."

He stopped writing to look up at Alfie. She was gritting her teeth. He laughed and went on. "She ain't no fit mother to no little girl 'less you was desirous of turning said girl into a woman of easy virtue." He looked up again. "How's that?"

"That'll do," Alfie said. "You can sign it."

Hagman toyed with the pencil for a moment, then put it down. "Let's get back to that apology."

Alfie forced a smile. "I'm sorry," she said in a sugary voice. "I shouldn't have called you a no-good bastard for giving Katherine to a whore. I probably shouldn't have kicked you in the shin."

"Probably?"

"Definitely."

"What else?"

"What else!" She nearly shrieked, then caught herself. Taking a deep breath, she went on, "I shouldn't have spit in your face, either."

Hagman grinned. "What should you have done?"

"What should I have done?"

Hagman nodded, obviously having a wonderful time, the bastard. Alfie's jaw was beginning to hurt. She wouldn't lose her temper. She needed that paper signed. She wanted something she could give to Brian that might help him get his girl back.

She breathed very slowly. She would tell him she should have realized he was just doing his job. Yes. That would sound placating without actually admitting that she thought he had done the right thing.

She opened her mouth but had to try twice before her voice was anything like she wanted it to be. "I should have . . . "

Hagman raised his eyebrows and nodded encouragingly, that stupid smile still on his face.

"I should have . . . I should have shot you when you came through the door, you dirty bloodsucker!"

Hagman roared with laughter. "I knew it. I knew you couldn't do it."

Alfie shook with fury, most of it directed at herself. She had failed. She saw little hope of salvaging the situation, but decided to wait until he finished laughing, then try to appeal to his sense of fair play. That was a long shot, certainly.

After what seemed like several minutes, he wiped tears from his eyes. "That was the most fun I've had in days."

Alfie's laugh was not intended to sound real. "Sign the paper, please."

"I ought to arrest you for impersonating a lady."

Alfie bit back a salty retort. Maybe if she stood here by his desk he would eventually get tired of looking at her and sign the paper to be rid of her.

Hagman chuckled again and lifted the pencil. "This may come as a surprise to you, but I didn't like taking that little girl away from you and giving her to Candy. 'Course, the way you act, makes me wonder if you're any more fit than she is." He grinned suddenly. "You're a sight more entertaining though."

To Alfie's amazement, he signed the document and handed it to her. It took her a second to collect herself enough to take it.

"I think I could get to like you, Miss Foster, but you have a strange effect on my deputies. See if you can stay outta trouble."

Alfie realized her mouth was hanging open. She snapped it shut and decided not to push her luck. Without another word, even the one of thanks she had briefly considered, she turned and left the office.

Brian's knock was answered by the impassive Rusty, who reminded him that they weren't open for business at that hour of the morning.

Brian shouldered past him. "I need to talk to Candy," he said with repressed fury. "Tell her I need to see my little girl."

"Tell Candy she has a visitor."

Brian turned to find Molly coming down the stairs. He glared at her as Rusty went to do her bidding.

"Won't you join me in the parlor, Mr. Reed?" She walked sedately in that direction without waiting to see if he followed.

Brian glanced up the stairs where Rusty had disappeared, toying with the idea of following him instead.

"Can I pour you a drink, Mr. Reed?" Molly called from the next room.

"No, thanks," Brian said, moving into the parlor.

The woman put the stopper back in the crystal bottle she had opened and sat down in one of the velvet chairs.

Brian regarded her for a moment, then asked, "Surely you can't approve of Candy's taking the child."

"It was you who brought her to us," she reminded him.

"But that was before. . . ."

"Before what? Before you knew what Candy did? I don't think so, Mr. Reed."

Brian turned away from her, running a hand through his hair. This was like some nightmare he had walked into. Or perhaps it was the last few days that had been the dream.

He spun back around to face Molly. "Do you intend to let the child grow up here?"

Molly shrugged. "I haven't really thought about it yet. Candy seems to think she'll be married soon."

A mirthless laugh escaped his lips before he could stop it. It was, of course, a possibility.

"I just want what's best for that little girl," he said, more to himself than to Molly.

"Really, Mr. Reed? Or do you want what's best for you?"

He took two strides toward her. "They're the same thing!"

He turned away from her and strode to the window, where he stood silently until Candy came to the door.

"Why, Mr. Reed, how charming of you to stop by to see me."

Brian glared at her. At least she was dressed this morning, though she seemed as tipsy as ever. "I need to see Katherine."

"You mean my little niece, Kat? I'm afraid

she can't come down." Candy made a beeline for the whiskey on the piano.

"Where is she?" Brian demanded.

"Oh, she's in her room," Candy said airily.

Brian stepped toward her, reminding himself he had to be calm. "I need to see her, to know she's all right."

"I think seeing you would upset her. She needs to get used to me now."

Brian supposed Candy's delicate sips of the whiskey were intended to make her look genteel. At ten in the morning, it made her look like a lush. He said, "You didn't want her until you learned about the money."

"Well, if I had known about the money at the beginning, I would have taken her then." Raising her voice she added, "And you would have left her."

The truth of that statement was like a blow to his gut. But that was before. "Listen. I don't care about the money. You can have it. I just want the girl."

Candy laughed. "Unfortunately for both of us, they go together."

Brian turned to leave, needing to get away from the woman before he lost his temper. At the door of the parlor a thought struck him. "I'll match it," he said. "Give me legal rights to the girl, and I'll pay you what her trust is worth."

"I don't think so," Candy said with another

laugh. "I looked into it. The girl's worth a quarter of a million dollars."

Brian left the house, bitterness rising in his throat until it threatened to choke him. Out in the street he turned and looked up at the house. Behind the sun's reflection in the glass of one of the upstairs windows, he thought he saw a small face. He stared at it, wanting to call out to Katie. As he started to raise his hand to wave to her, he saw her turn away.

Chapter Eleven

Brian walked slowly back to the hotel. He paused outside Alfie's door, knowing he should apologize for the way he had left her. But he couldn't face her yet. He wasn't ready for her sympathy or her logic. He needed some time alone.

He walked into his room next door, hearing an oppressive silence. One of Katherine's dresses was draped over the back of a chair, tossed there the evening before when she had changed into her nightgown before going to Alfie's. He touched it lightly with his fingertips.

Can you tie my bow. Daddy?

The vanity was covered with hair ribbons.

She never wore any except the blue ones after he'd told her it was his favorite color.

Alfie's eyes are blue, too, Daddy. Don't you think they're pretty?

He hadn't had the heart to tell her they were half the reason he liked blue so well. The other half was Katie's own eyes.

He felt as though he had lost them both, though Alfie was just next door. He had never held any real hope of keeping her though. She had her life, and he wasn't part of it. Knowing that had kept him from expecting too much, but it hadn't kept him from falling for her.

He'd had such dreams for Katie. Maybe all the more because he knew he would be losing Alfie. Had Katie been his consolation? Or was his love for her a separate issue altogether?

It didn't matter now, he thought, wandering around the room, touching each item that Katie had touched. They were both lost to him.

He should pack up all her things and have them sent to Molly's. He glared at the trunks that lined one wall. That would be giving up. That would be admitting to Candy and to Katie that he was relinquishing his hold on the girl. And he wasn't ready to do that. He couldn't leave her to a life with a woman who wanted her only for her inheritance!

Quickly he found paper and ink and began writing letters.

* * *

Alfie sealed the letter to her father's attorney and looked at the watch that was pinned to her white bodice. It was past noon. She should go ask Brian if he wanted to get some lunch, but she wasn't particularly hungry. She would wait for him to come to her.

An hour later, with her articles written and ready for the stage, she was still waiting. She was sure she had heard him come in shortly after she had. If he'd had any news he would have shared it with her, which meant he must not have been able to see Katherine.

There was another possibility she didn't like to consider. Perhaps he hadn't come to her because he blamed her. She had let Candy take his little girl. If he couldn't bear to be near her now, she could hardly blame him.

Knowing that Brian wouldn't have been able to stop Candy and Marshal Hagman either didn't keep her from feeling guilty. Last night, when she'd been lost in Brian's arms, he wasn't the one who'd forgotten about the child. He wasn't the one who had, for a moment or two, almost wished the girl away.

And her telling him that Candy might make a home for Katherine had sounded as if she were glad to have her gone. And she wasn't. She was missing her, too.

Another hour went by, and Alfie gave up hope that Brian would invite her to lunch. Fifteen minutes after that, she gave up hope that he would even come and talk to her. The stage was due soon and the sun was shining, so she took her letters and went to wait outside.

Once downstairs, she decided that a walk around town would appear less eccentric than pacing in front of the hotel, and sitting quietly was not a possibility. As she set a brisk pace down the boardwalk, she was conscious that every step took her farther away from Brian, when that was exactly where she wanted to run.

Brian wasn't quite finished with the last letter when he heard the stage pull into town. He knew he had about an hour before it pulled out again. He was seated by the window and gave the stage the barest glance as he continued to write to the Colorado territorial governor. Surely one of the letters he had written would inspire someone to intervene for a little girl.

As he blotted the last line of the letter, he glanced again out the window. Making her way briskly down the opposite sidewalk was Alfie. As he watched, she crossed the street and hurried to the stage.

She was leaving!

He hastily folded the last letter and addressed the envelope. He stuffed the stack of finished letters into his pocket and fanned the ink dry on the last one as he hurried from the room.

"Alfie!" He couldn't help shouting her name as he ran out of the hotel door.

He stood still, barely breathing, as he

watched her turn from talking to the stage driver. She looked at him only briefly before turning back for one last word; then she came in his direction. He wanted to go to meet her, but he was afraid. Afraid she was going to tell him she was leaving. Afraid he was going to beg her to stay.

"Is something wrong?" she asked.

"Are you leaving?"

She was close to him now, and the rest of the world dropped away. He waited for her answer to know if she was about to disappear as well.

"No," she whispered.

He let out the breath he had been holding and pulled her into his arms. He held her tightly until the sting in his eyes went away. "I thought you were leaving," he said softly.

"Brian," she said, drawing away enough to look up at him, "I wouldn't leave you like this."

The answer was reassuring only up to a point. She would eventually leave him.

"I was only sending some letters," she went on.

He nodded, gradually letting her go. "I have some as well. And a telegram for the driver to send. Have you eaten?" She shook her head. "Let me talk to the driver; then I'll buy you some lunch. Wait right here."

The driver had just unloaded the luggage from the top of the stage when Brian stopped him. During the few minutes it took to make his request, he found himself glancing over his shoulder at Alfie several times. He wasn't afraid she would disappear. He just found her uncommonly beautiful at the moment.

It might have been the way she stood, erect but at ease, or the way the sunlight shone in her golden hair. More likely only now, after coming so close to losing her, did he realize how precious she was.

Alfie waited on the boardwalk as Brian talked to the driver. His behavior of a moment before had been a surprise. A very pleasant, though unsettling, surprise. Did he care so much for her that the prospect of her leaving sent him chasing after her? Or was he counting on her help to get Katherine back?

As she thought of his warm embrace, she hoped it was the former, though it would probably be better if it was the latter. They had no future together. She didn't want him to be in love with her. They shouldn't both end up with broken hearts.

By silent agreement, they went down the street to a small café. Katherine's empty chair would be too conspicuous in the restaurant where they had shared several meals.

A short, round woman bustled out of the back when they entered. "It's a little late for lunch, folks," she said by way of greeting. "I've kept some soup bubbling, and I can always fry up some eggs."

"Soup is fine," Alfie said. Brian nodded his agreement and held a chair for her.

When the woman had returned to the kitchen, Alfie asked, "Did you get to see Katherine?"

Brian shook his head. "I talked to Candy. I offered to match the amount of the trust."

"You offered to buy her?" Why was she surprised?

Brian nodded. "But I can't. Unless you can loan me a quarter of a million."

"Brian, you can't just buy a child."

"Not at that price, anyway," he said.

Alfie decided not to press the point. "I wrote to my father's attorney. He might be able to help. I enclosed a letter from the marshal testifying to Aunt Candy's . . . line of work."

Brian blinked. "How did you get that?"

Alfie looked down at the scarred tabletop. "Let's just say it was humiliating and agree never to mention it again."

She looked up to find Brian staring at her, his eyes wide with shock. What he was thinking hit her a second later. "Oh, nothing like that!" she said with a shudder of disgust. "I . . . apologized."

Brian laughed, his relief evident. She wondered if he might have teased her about her apology if their hostess hadn't chosen that moment to bring them their steaming bowls of soup.

While they ate, Brian outlined the letters he

had sent. His associates at Reed Investigations were already trying to determine if there were any other family. "At first," he admitted as they left the café, "I was praying they wouldn't find any so that the way would be clear for me to adopt her. Now I'm praying they find someone. I can't leave her with that woman."

"What do we do now?" she asked.

"I don't know. Wait until we see what comes from our letters, I guess."

Wait? Alfie had never been good at waiting.

They walked the rest of the way to the hotel in silence. As they mounted the stairs Alfie said, "I keep picturing that shy little girl on the stage. She bloomed in your care, Brian."

He pulled her against his side but didn't speak.

"She has the doll," she went on. "She wouldn't leave without the doll. I keep wondering . . . " Her voice cracked and she bit her lip. She shouldn't be burdening Brian with her fears, anyway.

" . . . what she is doing now?" he finished, stopping in front of Alfie's door.

She nodded. "I'm sorry."

Brian pulled her into his arms. "I wonder, too," he whispered against her hair. "But children are resilient. And I won't leave her there any longer than I have to."

Alfie sighed, soaking up the comfort of his arms. But the comfort turned quickly to something else, something hot and demanding. A few more seconds like this, she realized, and she wouldn't be thinking of Katherine anymore. She pulled out of his arms, using the search through her reticule for her key as an excuse not to meet his eyes.

"Can I come in?" he whispered just as the lock clicked open.

She turned and saw her own desire reflected in his eyes. But was it really a good idea?

"My room's full of little dresses," he said.

She smiled gently, understanding how difficult that would be. She knew, too, that she was very close to a line that, once crossed, would allow no turning back. "Yes, come in," she whispered.

Brian closed the door behind them and leaned against it. He seemed a little uncomfortable, or maybe unsure of himself. Alfie wanted to laugh, but knew it was nerves. Or excitement. He had been here in the middle of the night while she was in her nightclothes and hadn't seemed so ill at ease.

But at those times he had been filled with excitement over ghost sightings or the latest in the murder cases. Now there was only sorrow and the hope of finding forgetfulness. And for Alfie, there was the very strong pull of desire for the man she loved.

While it was clear to Alfie what they both wanted, how to broach the subject wasn't so clear. The kisses they had shared had been completely spontaneous.

She walked farther into the room and turned so she could lean against the table. "I've been thinking," she said, glancing at him but not quite able to maintain eye contact. "We're both worldly people."

"Really?" he asked.

Alfie heard the humor in his voice and scowled at him. "Well, I want to be, at least. I want to travel all over, see the world and write about it."

"You like traveling?" he asked.

"You're not helping," she said.

He had taken a step or two toward her but stopped now. "Sorry," he said.

She watched as he removed his coat and tossed it toward the bed. The crisp white shirt hinted at, even as it hid, strong shoulders and a hard chest. She knew this for a fact, could still feel him pressed against her. She took a moment to reorganize her thoughts, which seemed to want to scatter. "Since we're both worldly people," she repeated, "I don't see any reason why we can't . . . "

Words failed her completely. *Well, darn it!* By now he should have caught on.

As soon as she met his eyes, he spoke. "Love each other?"

"I don't think we should love each other," she said, hearing her voice shake. How could it not shake, she wondered, when her stomach had an attack of butterflies? "Since you have your career and I have mine, and they aren't even in the same city, I don't think we should actually love each other."

He nodded in agreement. Somehow she found that very disappointing. How could he not love her? Oh, now she was being foolish. *Only now?* She wanted to laugh, but bit it back.

He took another slow step toward her. "You think we should make love to each other?"

She nodded. As his solid frame came even closer, the implications of what she had started hit her full force. Where had all these doubts been a few minutes ago? "Unless," she began, moving away from him before he had her trapped against the table. "Unless you think making love will make you fall in love. See, I don't think I want any complications, and heaven knows you don't need them either. And, you know, I would hate to think I broke someone's heart, when all I—"

"Be still a minute."

She hadn't considered that he could move so fast. Suddenly he was right in front of her and she was trapped by his nearness. His hands were on her shoulders, and she couldn't possibly pull away. The magnetism was too great. Even as his mouth was lowering to hers, she was leaning toward him.

She let him kiss her thoroughly, cooperating, of course, to the best of her ability. When he raised his head the arrogant smile on his face was fantastically appealing.

"You didn't let me make my point," she said just above a whisper.

He closed his eyes. "What *is* your point?"

"Promise me—" She broke off abruptly as he nibbled on her ear.

"Hmm?" he murmured.

She took it as encouragement to go on. "If we . . ."

"Make love," he said softly into her ear.

Oh, Lord, that sounded so tantalizing! Make love. As if what they were doing could win his love. No! That was what she was trying to prevent, wasn't she? "Promise me," she began again, choosing to ignore the laugh she was sure she heard, "if we . . . yes . . . uh . . . Promise me you won't fall in love with me."

He raised his head to look down at her. Those incredible warm brown eyes seemed to invite her to surrender. Which she was going to do, no matter what. In fact, to call this off, he would have to walk away. She wouldn't be the one to do it.

"I promise," he said very softly as he brushed a lock of hair away from her cheek and trailed his fingers around her ear and down her neck, then back around to her throat. "I won't fall in love with you."

Whyever not? she wanted to beg. She would have, but he chose to seal his statement with another kiss, and she didn't have the desire to push him away. By the time he paused, she was a little hazy on what she had wanted to say. All she was sure of was that his words had hurt her and she was miffed.

He began undoing the tiny pearl buttons on her bodice. The top three had already come loose by themselves. "What about you?"

It took Alfie a moment to realize what he was asking. "No, of course not," she said hastily. "I won't fall in love with you." And it was true. She wouldn't *fall* in love. It was far too late for that. She'd already fallen.

She had looked him straight in the eye as she had said it, hoping—by God, expecting—to see him flinch with disappointment at her declaration. Instead, he'd actually grinned.

She frowned, but he kissed her again. His kisses had the most disconcerting way of befuddling her brain. Even though she was sure she should be irritated at him, she still felt it only fair to help him off with his shirt. After all, he had removed hers with very little help on her part.

He seemed quite pleased with his handiwork, too, running his fingers under the edges of her chemise, skimming his tongue over her bare shoulders.

She, on the other hand, had come up against an undergarment that covered every bit as much as the shirt had. And this one wasn't coming off without his help.

"Brian?"

"Hmm?" He moved his mouth to the tender flesh just under her ear.

She savored the sensations for a few seconds before she continued. "I need some help here," she said finally, giving his undershirt a good tug.

"Oh, sorry." He doffed the shirt in a second and got back to her neck.

Yes, this was nice. Firm muscles rippled under warm, smooth skin and soft, springy hair. What a wonderful treat for her fingers. He must have enjoyed her exploration as well, for she heard a low groan when her fingers trailed across the hard buds of his nipples.

She tried to take a step closer to him and found her skirts and petticoats pooled around her feet. She was rather impressed with his dexterity at having gotten them there without her knowing. Of course, she had been otherwise occupied.

She ducked away from Brian to step out of the skirts and discovered the ribbons were all undone on her chemise and it was about to slip off her shoulders. He had been busy. In another moment she would have been wearing nothing but her drawers and he was still . . .

She found him watching her with his hands on his hips. He didn't look particularly happy. She fought the urge to giggle.

"You're still half-dressed," she said, pulling the loose chemise back into place, though she knew it covered precious little. She told herself she should be mortified, but this was Brian.

"Is that why we stopped?" he asked.

"My skirts were in my way." Then she realized what he must be thinking. "You thought I was . . . chickening out?"

"I wouldn't call it that. If you want to quit—"

"No," she said, coming toward him, kicking the skirts aside as she passed.

"Good," he said, wrapping her in his arms. "I wouldn't call you chicken," he murmured directly in her ear, "but I might call you a tease."

She giggled, more from the sensation of his breath in her ear than at what he said.

He stood up straight, pinning her with his deep brown eyes. She sobered immediately. Very slowly he let his hands slide down her arms, forcing them to drop to her sides. The chemise, she discovered with little surprise, went with his hands. Then his hands moved to her waist and slid the flimsy garment along with her drawers down her hips, down her thighs, and finally to the floor.

For half a second she wondered when he had loosened the ribbons on her drawers, but the question seemed a little irrelevant. Especially since the rest of him had followed his hands down her body and he was now placing kisses on her lower abdomen, shockingly close to the triangle of curls at the place she had never shared with anyone.

Instinctually she tried to press her knees together, but with her senses already overwrought, she found them trembling instead. She thought she ought to warn Brian that she was about to collapse, but only a murmur passed her lips.

Then she uttered a gasp as she found herself hoisted into the air, supported by Brian's strong arms. He laid her on the bed and planted a possessive kiss on her lips. "Wait right here," he said.

He straightened and worked the buttons on his pants loose. She reached one hand tentatively toward him. She had planned to do that, had looked forward to it, in fact. But then she had been distracted. By what? *Oh, yes!* A shiver ran down her body, following the path of his hands as he had stripped off the last of her garments.

For a second she closed her eyes in pleasure, then opened them again, not wanting to miss watching Brian as he disrobed. But he had gotten no farther than removing his belt when he sat on the edge of the bed to take off his shoes.

That was when she realized she was still wearing hers, along with her stockings. It struck her as funny. She sat up, scooting over beside him, intending to take them off. She felt a little light-headed and leaned against him instead.

He kissed her soundly, laying her back onto the bed again. "I told you not to move," he said.

"No, you didn't," she argued. "My shoes." She raised one of her legs, which hung over the bed. He stood and caught it, then removed her shoes.

"That's better," she said saucily, stretching on the bed. But just as she relaxed, he decided to torture her, rolling her stockings down her calves, one tiny fraction at a time. By the time he slipped them off her toes, she was gasping for breath again, feeling oddly impatient.

"Brian?" she whispered.

In a moment he was hovering over her. "Yes, my sweet?"

She wrapped her arms around his neck and brought him down on top of her. The weight of his body pressing her into the soft mattress was surprisingly delicious. He kissed her quickly, and, when he would have pulled away, she held him fast, delving her tongue into his mouth to convey her own urgency.

She would have liked to roll him onto his back, but she didn't have the strength. She settled for wrapping one leg, the one that wasn't trapped, around his backside. The fabric felt rough against her recently sensitized calf.

"Patience," he murmured and drew away.

She went with him, letting him lift her to a sitting position, before she unwound her arms from his neck. "Now who's the tease?"

His thumbs in his waistband, he started to turn away from her. "No, no," she whispered.

She wiggled her fingers, hoping to entice him to step closer. He didn't comply. In fact, he looked a little startled. "Don't be shy," she teased. "You can see every inch of me."

"I was trying to protect your delicate sensibilities," he said with a grin. "I should have known better."

Then he did it. He slid his trousers and underdrawers down his hips, freeing his proud male member to her sight. All the books on ancient art had not quite prepared Alfie for the size of him or for the instant curl of anticipation the sight of him produced within her.

She didn't realize she was staring until he cleared his throat. "Are you frightened?" he asked.

She looked up, startled. "That hadn't occurred to me. Should I be?" But this was Brian. Of course she wasn't.

"That depends," he said.

But she didn't believe him. She could only imagine him buried deep inside her, easing an ache that was becoming unbearable.

"This is your first time?" he asked.

"Yes," she answered absently. If he wasn't going to come to her, she would have to go get him. But she wasn't sure her legs would hold her. She reached toward him, and he took the hint. She shifted on the bed to make room for him.

As he settled over her he whispered, "I'll be gentle."

Well, of course he would. She ran her nails over his bare back. She wasn't sure she wanted gentle, anyway. She was throbbing with need, and there wasn't anything gentle about that.

Brian trailed kisses down her neck, across her breastbone and finally onto the peak of one of her breasts. The sensation felt so exquisitely wonderful, it should have overshadowed the fire burning lower within her body, but instead it somehow intensified it.

He continued this new form of torture, dividing his interest between her breasts until she felt she was wound so tightly that she would snap. Finally, he tended to that fire itself, and he slid inside until he met the barrier she knew to fear.

But Alfie thought she would explode if he stopped now. She wrapped both legs around him and arched toward him, taking him deep inside with a burst of pleasure-pain that made her cry out with the power of it.

Then she did explode, sending shock waves through her body, one after another, until she lay limp and panting, quivering with contentment.

"God." The stunned whisper was almost directly in her ear.

She should feel stunned, too, she thought with a smile, except she didn't have the energy. In fact, she imagined that she no longer even had bones. She would probably never move again.

She felt Brian slowly withdraw, almost entirely, then settle inside her again. Her body, which she had thought entirely spent, began to tense once more in anticipation of a release greater than before. Over and over he repeated the motion, driving faster and deeper each time.

The second explosion, when it came, was triggered by his convulsions and answered by her own. This time it took her a moment to settle back down to earth.

Brian rolled off her and lay as still as she. Alfie wanted to laugh or cry, it had been so wonderful. Instead, she heaved a huge sigh.

After just a few minutes, her body began to return to normal. Yet she knew she would never be the same. She smiled to herself and, for the moment, banished any thought of regrets. She rolled to her side, propping herself up on one elbow, and watched as the man she loved slept.

Chapter Twelve

Brian opened one eye to find Alfie displaying an avid interest in parts of his anatomy that should have had her blushing pink. Perhaps she was, he thought. Her whole body had a rosy glow, warm and inviting. He grabbed her, eliciting a startled cry from her shapely lips, and brought her down on top of him.

"I thought you were asleep," she said with a gasp.

"With your eyes burning into me like that?" He gathered the soft hair that fell around her face like a satin curtain.

"You can't feel somebody's eyes on you," she said, squirming in a most arousing fashion.

It didn't seem productive to argue. Coaxing

her lips towards his was a better use of energy. Soft, pliable lips. And a most inquisitive tongue. Yes, he thought a moment later, he had made the right choice. This was much better than arguing.

After a few tentative kisses, Alfie seemed to enjoy having the upper hand. Brian definitely didn't mind. By the time she realized the extent of the possibilities of their positioning, he was more than ready to accommodate her.

Later, after they had satiated themselves fully, Brian pulled a blanket over them both and settled her head onto his shoulder. He pushed his doubts and fears to the back of his mind and concentrated, instead, on the pleasure of his satiated body and Alfie's warm flesh beside him.

Brian awoke alone in bed at twilight. Lying still for a moment, he assured himself that he hadn't been dreaming. He and Alfie had come together with a shockingly explosive intensity. If she thought she could just walk away, she had a lot to learn about what it meant to fall in love.

He sat up to find her silhouetted against the feeble light of the window. She turned toward him when the bed creaked.

"It's late," she said softly. "Are you hungry?"

"Yeah," he answered, swinging his legs over the side of the bed, "but I'm afraid you'll be sore in the morning."

A long moment of silence was followed by a muttered, "I meant for food."

Brian's clothes had been spread across the foot of the bed, a hint, he supposed, that he should get dressed. He found his pants and pulled them on, leaving the rest. With a match from his pocket, he lit the lamp on the table. "I wasn't completely honest with you," he said.

She looked up at him. He turned the lamp down to a soft glow. It seemed more fitting for the conversation. He sat in the chair across from her.

"What do you mean?" she asked.

"You've got to understand, Alfie, that a man's willing to promise almost anything to get . . . what you gave me." He tipped his head toward the bed slightly and watched her glance toward it.

She sat up a little straighter. "But you didn't promise me anything."

"Yes, I did."

She frowned and shook her head.

"I promised not to fall in love with you."

She closed her eyes and turned away.

"I didn't lie, Alfie," he continued, willing her to look at him. "I was already in love with you."

She didn't move.

"And furthermore, I think you're in love with me."

She turned then. "What? Of all the arrogant—"

He raised a hand and said softly, "You told me."

"No, I didn't!" She came to her feet.

"The first time you kissed me."

She placed her hands on the table and leaned toward him. She likely had no idea how appealing she looked, the effect of the prim white collar ruined by the waves of golden hair that fell around her shoulders. He tried not to grin but failed.

She opened her mouth, which looked very kissable, then closed it, narrowing her eyes.

"Arrogant?" he prompted.

It must have been what she needed to find her voice. "A woman can kiss a man without being in love with him. A man wouldn't be able to tell one way or the other. And furthermore," she said, evidently intending to throw his words back in his face, "I don't believe you're in love with me." She straightened and folded her arms across her chest.

"No?"

"No."

He came slowly to his feet. "I can prove it."

She put out a hand to stop him. "You won't prove anything except what you said earlier. A man will say anything to get . . . "

She had glanced toward the bed as her voice trailed off. Her expression seemed to soften ever so slightly.

He stepped close enough to take her raised

hand and press it against his bare chest. "You were saying?"

Her attention was riveted on his hands, which held hers captive. Her lips parted and she leaned slightly toward him. He moved in to claim a kiss, but she broke away.

She was halfway across the room before she turned to face him. "We can't be in love with each other. Soon, maybe even tomorrow, one or both of us will leave this town, and we'll never see each other again. It would be silly to fall in love."

Brian let the silence stretch between them. When she started to fidget, he spoke. "So just like that, you can talk yourself out of it?"

She glared at him.

"Is that how you kept from loving Katie?"

Her lips trembled, but she said, "Yes."

"I see." He walked slowly toward her. When she started to ease away, he turned toward his clothes instead. "You want to get dinner?"

"What?"

He knew the change of subject was abrupt, but he was too drained to argue. He had some time, at least until the stage came the next afternoon, to change her mind. He pulled his undershirt over his head. "What time is it? Do you think the dining room's still open?"

She didn't answer.

"I don't know about you," he said, slipping on his shirt, "but I worked up an appetite."

He was hoping she would at least blush, but she simply watched him. With an inward sigh, he finished dressing.

"You're *not* in love with me," she said.

"No?" He straightened his suit coat and reached a hand toward her, wanting to take her arm and escort her out the door.

"*No.*" she said, not moving toward him. "You used me to forget about Katherine for a time."

He thought about stepping toward her, but wanted her to come to him. He didn't lower his arm, merely flexed his fingers. "Are you comfortable with that?"

A frown creased her brow. "Yes," she said after a moment. "Because I used you for the same reason."

He didn't believe her. That was why he was able to muster a smile. Two steps and he took her arm. "I thought you said you didn't love Katie, either."

Her frown deepened, and she didn't move. "I can miss her without loving her."

"Let's go get dinner," he said, urging her toward the door.

Early morning light streamed through the window, but Alfie didn't see any reason to get up. She pulled the covers over her head instead. She'd had a terrible night. First she'd felt guilty for sending Brian off to his own room with its memories of Katherine. Then she'd crawled into bed and discovered it had a few memories of its own, and she'd wished she had invited him in for quite a different reason.

As the night had worn on it had become impossible not to think about Katherine. The poor little girl was probably scared, maybe even being mistreated. Was she warm? Had she been fed? Was she sleeping soundly with her doll tucked in her arm, or was she crying for her daddy?

Alfie was certain that she'd had only a few hours of sleep when the light awakened her. Even with the blanket forming a relatively dark cocoon, sleep had been practically impossible.

She tried thinking about going back to Denver and her job, and found herself feeling depressed. Her boss was every bit as pigheaded as Marshal Hagman, yet at least that man had turned out to have a sense of humor. Imagining herself calling her boss the names she had called the marshal brought a smile to her lips for a moment. But then she remembered the rest of the incident, and she was back to thinking about Katherine.

She should get up, she told herself. She should get dressed. Just what she would do after that, she had no idea. So she stayed in bed and counted sheep, named the presidents, tried to name the states in order of admission to the union, and finally found herself getting drowsy again.

"Alfie!" The loud whisper was followed by a knocking on her door.

With a groan, she crawled out of bed and let Brian in.

"Look at this," he said, seemingly unfazed.

He thrust a folded newspaper under her nose but continued to hold it as if he planned to read it over her shoulder. It required him to practically press himself against her. Practically. She had to lean back for it to actually happen. She wasn't sure he noticed.

"I went down to the newspaper office this morning to see what they had to say about the sale of Winter's Gate. Here's the article. It says Jason Wingate's going to manage the mine. And look at this." With an enticing shift of his body, he was looking over her other shoulder and a flyer replaced the newspaper. "These had just been printed up."

She took the flyer and stepped away, knowing she wouldn't make heads or tails of it as long as she was in Brian's embrace. "They're advertising for miners. So?"

"It says the murders have been solved." He moved behind her to point at the smaller print. "The mine is safe again."

"How can they claim the murders have been solved?"

"I found that in here, too." This time he wrapped both arms around her as he refolded the paper. " 'Witness found.' Read that."

She took the paper and skimmed the article. "Witness to murders comes forward . . . saw large man . . . afraid for own safety . . . Murderer has left the area." She lowered the paper. "Do you think it's true?"

"No." He pointed over her shoulder. "Look who the witness is. Albert Thurston. I talked to Thurston. He didn't witness anything."

"Maybe it's not the same man."

"Maybe. But I'd sure like to talk to him."

Alfie handed the newspaper back and moved to sit on the bed. "Brian, I can't get excited about this. It just doesn't seem to matter, all else considered."

He knelt in front of her. "If I can prove Wingate or Kline paid Thurston to make these statements, I'm on my way to proving a conspiracy to take the mine."

Alfie couldn't believe he even cared about the mine anymore. He had been fired. "So what? This has nothing to do with your ghost. And nothing to do with Katherine."

"But it does," he said, his enthusiasm seemingly undampened. "At least with Katherine. If I can prove Candy's part of the conspiracy, she won't get to keep Katie."

"You're not making sense." She said it gently, hoping he'd realize his logic had taken one leap too far. She resisted the temptation to run her fingers through his hair. She'd want to pull his head into her lap, and, of course, she could imagine where things would go from there.

"Jason was in Candy's room when he shot at me."

She gazed for a moment into his clear brown

eyes. Maybe it wasn't his logic that was faulty. Maybe it was his expectations. "How do you plan to prove anything, Brian?"

While that didn't exactly take the wind out of his sails, it at least slowed him down. He rose and paced the room, making her want to call him back.

"I don't know. But I can start with Thurston."

"All you will prove is that Jason and Kline are willing to print up lies to get the mine back into operation. It won't implicate Candy in any way."

He took a deep breath. "Then I'll get a job at the mine and see what I can learn."

Alfie tried to picture Brian shoveling a carload of blasted rock but had trouble. There was more than just hard work facing him. "Have you ever been in a mine?"

"No," he said, a touch of resentment showing. "Have you?"

"Yes," she said, surprising him. "I sneaked in to write a story on one once. In most mines, you climb into what amounts to a cage and they drop you a few hundred feet underground. Sometimes you're perched on makeshift scaffolding, working on a rock face over your head."

He looked away. During the stagecoach ride, she'd noticed his reaction. He had a fear of heights. She didn't want to mention it outright and hoped she had said enough to deter him.

With a sigh he crossed to a chair by the window and sat down, putting his head in his hands. "I'm open to other suggestions," he muttered.

She rose slowly and moved to join him. He sat up and wrapped his arms around her hips, resting his head against her stomach. She caressed his hair, his face, feeling the tension in his jaw. "Maybe there'll be some news on the stage."

"Some miracle?" he asked, looking up at her with a forced smile.

"Exactly." She pulled him back against her.

Alfie wasn't hungry, but she forced herself to go down for lunch with Brian. It went much as dinner had the night before. The waiter, having heard of their loss, or perhaps actually having overheard Alfie's confrontation with Marshal Hagman, seated them at a tiny table and refrained from smiling in their presence.

The hours before the arrival of the stage seemed to last forever. Alfie wished she could tumble into bed with Brian and forget everything the way they had the evening before, but Brian wouldn't stop pacing long enough for her to catch him. It wasn't a good idea anyway, she reminded herself. It had made him declare his love for her.

So Alfie tried to write another article on the mine, and Brian paced. At one point, Alfie's nerves became too tense to handle the distraction. "Why don't you go pace in your own room?" she asked.

"Sorry." He sat down on her unmade bed.

That, she decided, was even more distracting. "You could go try to find this Thurston fellow."

"I doubt if I can until nighttime. He works in one of the mines." He looked up and suspiciously met her gaze. "Are you trying to get rid of me?"

She sighed. "I'm trying to write an article." She couldn't help but smile.

"All right," he said, moving toward her. "You can turn me out to go wandering around town. I'll probably be set upon by thieves, or maybe even fall in with thieves." He kissed her possessively. "My life, such as it is, will be ruined, if not actually lost, but you'll get your article written."

"Have fun," she said.

He left, but the article didn't write any smoother and the stage didn't come any faster. Long before it arrived, she had folded the article and addressed it to her editor, knowing it needed more work but not caring. Within minutes she was following Brian's path back and forth across her room.

When she heard the rumble and jingle of the stage coming in, she was out the door and in the street before the coach stopped rocking. "Please, please," she whispered as she watched the three passengers disembark. She waited a moment longer, hoping against hope that there would be one more passenger. The driver slammed the door shut and climbed to the top to unload.

Until that moment, she hadn't realized how much she had hoped her father's attorney would be on the stage. She had imagined him getting her letter, running straight to a judge's office to get the proper papers, and catching the stage this morning. But she wouldn't give up hope until she saw what might be in the mail.

Brian came to stand beside her, his arm around her waist giving her strength. He smelled of fresh mountain air with a touch of wood smoke.

"Did you meet any thieves?" she asked.

"My new friends? They're waiting over there."

Alfie looked where he indicated. A group of four tough-looking men seemed to be watching him. She turned questioning eyes to Brian. He grinned down at her.

She didn't get to question him further. The driver had produced the mailbag and turned it over to Helen, who served as Glitter Creek's postmistress. The driver came back to stand in front of Alfie and Brian.

"I got an answer to your telegram," he said, drawing a folded paper out of his pocket.

"Thanks." Brian took the paper and opened it. Alfie felt a chill run up her back. What if it was bad news?

She watched Brian fold the note and put it in his pocket. "Well?"

"Katie has no other relatives, or so her grandmother's attorney has assured my associates. Let's see if we have any mail."

They waited impatiently as the mail was sorted. In the end there was only one letter, a brief note to Alfie from her father's attorney. He was willing to help with adoption proceedings, but, he wrote, these things took time.

They started up the stairs to their rooms, but Brian stopped abruptly. "I'm going to try again to see Katie. If nothing else, I'll camp across the street in case she comes to a window."

"That would be approximately where you were when Jason shot at you."

"Give or take a few feet," he said, turning to leave.

Alfie sighed. She watched until he was out the door, then turned to follow.

San Francisco Street was quiet. They found a backless bench in front of one of the saloons and moved it up the street until it was across from Molly's. "There's the bullet," Brian said conversationally as they sat down on the bench.

Alfie looked at the indentation and splintered wood on the side of the building. "You were lucky."

"Maybe I should take up poker after all." He grinned down at her. "I got lucky yesterday, too."

Alfie turned away, deciding not to admit that

she understood what he meant. "Which window?"

He pointed. "That one, I think. I thought I saw a face there yesterday. The morning sun was reflecting off the glass, so I couldn't be sure."

"Maybe they let her play downstairs during the day," Alfie said, imagining the poor child confined to one room.

"I'm more concerned about where she is in the evenings," Brian said.

Alfie had thought about Katie last night, too, but the hard tone of Brian's voice startled her. It took a second for her to understand. "Surely her aunt isn't still . . . working!"

"I don't know."

They were silent after that, watching a house that might well have been deserted. After a long stretch of time, they saw a face appear at an upstairs window.

Alfie caught her breath. "Katherine?"

Brian didn't answer. He didn't need to. Katherine had moved close enough to the glass that they could see her clearly now. Her doll was in the crook of her arm, and she gave them a little wave with her fingertips.

Alfie felt tears burn her eyes. The child was so close it seemed as if she ought to be able to run across the street and get her. In reality, she was well beyond their reach, at least at the moment.

Knowing she would cry if she looked at

Katherine for another moment, Alfie turned toward Brian. He was attempting to smile at the girl, but his eyes were moist and red.

"We know she's all right," Alfie said gently. "And she knows we haven't forgotten her."

"I want her to know more than that." Brian came to his feet, cupping his hands around his mouth. "Katie!" he shouted. "Katie, I love you!"

Windows and doors flew open up and down the quiet street, followed by muttered curses.

Katherine knocked on her window and shouted something that they couldn't understand. A moment later she was pulled away from the window, and a shade came down to hide the room.

"We should go," Alfie said, after a couple of minutes of staring at the drawn shade.

Brian shook his head, sitting back on the bench. "She might peek around the shade. I want to still be here."

Several minutes passed before the front door of the building opened and a large man stepped out.

"Rusty," Brian said.

"That's just great," Alfie said angrily, needing to vent the tension that had been building all day. "It's important to be on a first-name basis with the man who's going to kill you."

"That's what I thought," Brian said mildly.

The big man stopped in the street in front of them. "You're going to have to leave."

"I'm sorry. Do you own this bench?"

Rusty scowled. "If you don't leave I'm going to get the marshal."

Brian smiled. "I'm sorry to make you walk all the way up those stairs, Rusty, but we're not leaving."

Rusty glared at them and turned to go.

"Unless," Brian said, stopping him, "you bring that little girl down here so we can talk to her."

Rusty turned away and lumbered down the street.

Alfie sighed. At least they had gotten to see Katherine. When Brian made no move to rise, she asked, "Are we just going to wait here for the marshal?"

Brian didn't answer.

"I've enjoyed the marshal's hospitality once already," she said. "I'm not crazy about a second visit."

He turned toward her. "You can leave if you want to."

She studied his eyes, unable to tell if he would be disappointed if she did just that. "And miss your little talk with the marshal? Not likely."

The street settled into its earlier quiet. Though Alfie saw the shade stir a couple of times, her thoughts became occupied with the man beside her. He was crazy, but he wasn't stupid. Surely he would leave when the marshal came. He had gotten his point across to Katherine and to her aunt; he wouldn't be giving up. Sitting here the rest of the afternoon wouldn't make that much difference.

When she heard footfalls on the hard-packed street, she knew it was Marshal Hagman. Rusty angled across the street and reentered the house, casting a frown in their direction before he closed the door.

"Good afternoon, Marshal," Brian said.

"Well, boy, how good it is remains to be seen."

"You're kidding!" Brian sounded truly surprised. "Look at that blue sky. Smell that air."

Alfie stole a peek at a cloud that chose that moment to block the sun. It would be raining in a matter of minutes. The temperature had dropped about five degrees.

Brian continued undaunted, "It's a wonderful day to just sit back and relax." He leaned against the building behind them, his feet crossed at the ankles, looking for all the world as if he intended to take a nap.

"I've had a complaint against you for disturbing the peace."

"The peace doesn't seem disturbed to me," Brian said without opening his eyes.

Alfie stole a glance at Hagman. He looked about as annoyed as she'd expected. She mentally tallied what was left of her father's money in case she had to pay bail to have Brian released.

"Look," Hagman said, moving around to stand directly in front of Brian, "Rusty says you was making noise, and I believe him. Now if you—"

"If noise is against the law, you should come down here at night."

Hagman cleared his throat. "If you leave now, I won't arrest you."

Brian appeared to be thinking it over. Alfie wished she knew of something to aid his cause, but she wasn't exactly on the marshal's good side. Anything she said might be held against Brian.

"No," Brian said at length, "I don't think you have grounds to arrest me. I guess I'll stay right here."

Hagman sighed. "It ain't that I don't understand what you're doing. I sympathize; I surely do. But you can't sit here and watch the house. It's making the ladies nervous."

Brian opened his eyes. "Ladies?"

"Look, Reed, either you move along, or I'll arrest Miss Foster." With that as his only warning, he grabbed Alfie's arm and jerked her off the bench and into the street beside him.

"On what grounds?" Brian shouted, coming to his feet.

Once she had caught her balance, Alfie's reaction to Hagman's manhandling was to try to pry his hand loose.

"Resistin' arrest," Hagman said, grinning. Alfie's small foot connected with his shin. "Assaultin' an officer."

Alfie tried punching him. "Damn it, Hagman, get your hands off me!"

"Swearin'," Hagman added mildly.

"Let her go," Brian ordered. "We'll leave."

"Good," Hagman said, giving Alfie a shove that sent her into Brian's arms. "I didn't really want her in my jail, anyway. She scares my deputy. Why don't you go on about your business and quit causing me trouble?"

Brian's arms wrapped protectively around Alfie. After a moment during which Alfie imagined him glaring at Hagman, he started toward the stairs. "Are you all right?" he whispered.

"Fine." Alfie felt guilty. Hagman's tactics were typical of the man. In fact, she should have expected them. Perhaps if she had left, Brian might have stared him down. "I'm sorry," she said.

"Hagman found my weakness."

She looked up to find him smiling. He turned her in his arms and gave her what could only be described as a possessive kiss. "I wanted to kill him when he touched you," he said. "I could go back and sock him, if you want me to."

Alfie resisted the urge to see if Hagman was watching them. "I don't think that would be a good idea."

"But he probably bruised your arm." He ran his hand gently over the offended limb.

"I probably bruised his shin," she responded.

He grinned again. "Good for you."

It was very pleasant being held so close and having him look at her so adoringly. "Brian?"

"What, Alfie?" His mouth hovered over hers, promising a more thorough kiss.

She tried for her most seductive voice. "Take me back to the hotel."

His eyes widened and he pulled her a fraction closer.

The first raindrops hit them as she added, "Before Hagman arrests us for public indecency."

Chapter Thirteen

Alfie had let him spend the night. He hadn't been sure she would. He could no longer use Katie's things as an excuse to stay in Alfie's room; she had helped him pack them up. Not that he intended to send them to Candy. They would be ready when he took Katie away from Glitter Creek. Though when and how he would do that were still unknown.

While they'd packed up the little dresses, he and Alfie had talked through several possibilities. The best plan seemed to be to return to Denver and enlist the help of the attorney who had written to Alfie.

But Brian hated to do it. What if Candy took

the girl away while they were gone? What if he couldn't find her?

His mind reasoned that they could trace her through the estate. Candy would have to let the grandmother's attorney know where she was in order to get the money. His heart broke at the thought of not knowing where his little girl was, even for a moment.

After dinner he had gone in search of Thurston. The man he had interviewed his first evening in town was indeed the Albert Thurston mentioned in the newspaper article. He hadn't been around to his usual watering holes. He hadn't, in fact, even gone to work today. Brian learned where the man lived and found the room had been vacated. Another dead end.

So, although he had recently made love to the most attractive, most imaginative, and most loving woman in the world, he couldn't sleep. And that was why he was awake to hear the light footfalls past the door, the feminine whisper, and a knock farther down the hall.

He crept quietly out of bed and slipped into his drawers. He eased the door open. A young woman was indeed outside the door to his room, whispering his name. In a moment, he recognized her as the woman who had greeted him so aggressively at Molly's his first day in town. "Honey?"

He heard Alfie stir behind him as the young woman hurried toward him, pushed him inside the room, and closed the door. "I guess I had the wrong room," she said.

"Not necessarily," Brian muttered. "What are you doing here, Honey?"

"Honey?" Alfie sounded annoyed.

The new arrival's attention shifted to the bed. "Well, shoot!" She gave Alfie a pouty glare.

Brian wanted to assure Alfie that he could explain, but he wasn't sure that was true. "I met her at Molly's whorehouse" didn't seem like a wise thing to say.

"Oh, well." Honey sighed and plopped down at the foot of the bed. Alfie, the sheet wrapped around her breasts, scooted away from her.

Brian considered lighting a lamp, but he wasn't sure he wanted a better look at either woman's face. He was sure that he didn't want them getting a better look at his. The moonlight would have to do.

"I came to tell you about Candy and the girl," Honey said rather petulantly. "You were going to be so grateful."

"I am grateful," Brian said, stepping toward her. "What can you tell us?"

With another sigh, she began. "Candy and Jason had a big fight. He took her and the girl away."

"Away! Where?" Brian placed his hands on her shoulders, trying to read her eyes in the dim light.

"Brian."

Alfie's voice made him jump as if he'd been burned.

"Get dressed," Alfie said. He watched her slip out of bed and toss the sheet aside. She was beautifully naked, the moonlight gleaming on her skin. He was too surprised to do anything but stare.

"You," she said, indicating Honey. "Tell us everything you know."

"Sure, all right." Honey seemed only momentarily startled by Alfie's lack of modesty. She was likely used to seeing women undressed. "Candy's had this thing for Jason since forever. I always thought he was just stringing her along, but she swore he'd marry her someday. First she'd blamed his old man for it not happening; then she figured—"

"Speed this up a little," Alfie said. She was almost fully clothed, and Brian hadn't managed to move.

"Oh, sure. Well, now that she has some money, she was sure he wouldn't refuse her. But he has the mine and doesn't need her money anymore. Candy knew all about some scheme to get the mine from the old man. I don't know the details, but tonight, when he still refused to marry her, she said she'd go to the law with what she knew if he didn't go through with it."

Brian met Alfie's eyes. His theory had been right. Candy was in on the whole thing. She pointed toward his clothes, and he hurried to get dressed.

"I almost laughed out loud at that," Honey went on. "The law was just down the hall."

"And where were you?" Brian asked, pushing his arms through the sleeves of his undershirt.

Honey rose from the bed and came toward him, making him wish he hadn't called attention to himself. "Why, I was just outside of Candy's door," Honey cooed.

She helped him pull his shirt down and started to tuck it into his drawers. He caught her hands. "Why don't you see if Alfie needs help with her dress?"

Alfie snorted, but Honey shrugged and moved away. Brian hoped neither woman heard his sigh of relief.

"Kat—that's what Candy calls the little girl—Kat was supposed to wait in the kitchen since Candy had a customer, but she forgot her doll and ran back for it. I was in the parlor and saw her start up the stairs. I ran to stop her and caught up with her just outside the door. It was ajar. The girl must have started to open it, then heard the fighting and froze. I tried to coax Kat away, but she kept whispering something about Daddy's dolly and wouldn't move. That's how I overheard so much."

"What else did you overhear?" Alfie asked. She sat down on the bed and efficiently pulled on her stockings. Brian found himself distracted until she dropped the skirt back in place.

"Jason said he'd had enough of her threats. All he ever wanted her for was a good time and she was ruining that.

"Then, all of a sudden, he agreed. Just like that he said he'd marry her. I didn't believe him, but evidently Candy did. I heard the door start to open, so I ran down the hall and hid in a doorway. Little Kat just stood there."

"You left her?" Alfie asked, stomping into a shoe.

"I didn't know what else to do." Honey looked at Brian for reassurance. "At least I escaped to come to you."

"I'm glad you did," Brian said, not daring to look at Alfie for fear she'd think he was condoning Honey's behavior. He simply wanted the woman calm enough to tell them everything. "Did he take Katie, too?"

Honey nodded. "He came out of the room with his arm around Candy. When he saw the little girl, he laughed and said she should come, too. She tried to run but he caught her."

Brian was completely dressed now. He checked his pocket for his gun and made sure it was loaded. "Can you tell us where they went?"

"He took them to the livery," she said. "I followed long enough to see that; then I came up here."

Brian's gut told him that if Wingate was getting rid of a blackmailer, the logical place would be one of the old mine tunnels. He prayed he was right.

Alfie, ready at nearly the same moment as Brian, met him at the door. Honey followed more slowly. While Brian waited for Alfie to lock the door, Honey slithered up against him. He tried to ease away but nearly lost his balance. She moved along with him, wrapping her leg around his. "What can I do to help?" she whispered.

Alfie answered for him. "Go get Hagman out of bed and tell him what you told us."

Honey reluctantly walked away, swinging her hips a little more than could possibly be necessary.

Alfie cleared her throat, and Brian gave her an apologetic glance. He took her arm and hurried her toward the stairs.

"Horses will be faster than a buggy," Alfie said. "I can ride."

"We don't even know where he's going," Brian said.

"I'm hoping the man at the livery can tell us. It'll be light soon," Alfie said as they hurried down the street. "That should help." The sky above the eastern peaks still looked dark.

The liveryman was unhappy at being roused by more customers. "Second time tonight," he grumbled.

Brian followed him to help saddle the horses. "Jason Wingate was here."

"Yeah, Wingate. He boards his own horse here, but he wanted to rent a buggy 'cause of the folks with him."

Brian wished the man wouldn't quit working when he talked. Still he needed all the information he could get. "Did Wingate say where he was going?"

The liveryman scratched his head. "Said he had to get the little girl to a doctor. 'Twas his excuse for gettin' me up in the middle of the night." He cast Brian a sour look, indicating he'd heard no reasonable excuse from them. Brian ignored it. "The girl was havin' fits or something. Kept screaming for him to let her go."

Brian felt his stomach churn. If Wingate had hurt his little girl . . . "Did you see which way they headed?"

"Happen to know they turned left out them doors."

Brian thought the mine was still his best bet. But that could mean anywhere on Wingate's side of the mountain. Chances were good that no one had seen him leave town, or at least no one he would be able to locate in time.

Alfie heard the liveryman tell Brian that Jason had rented a buggy. With that bit of information, she went back to the big double doors and inspected the ground. The street itself was a mess of ruts and holes, as usual. Yesterday's shower had filled the holes with water and made the new tracks deeper. Only one set of wheels had left the livery since the rain.

She heard Brian behind her and said, "The mud's slowing the buggy down." She pointed to the deep cuts in the street. "We may even be able to follow their tracks."

"I'll leave that to you," he said, helping her into the saddle. "I'm a city boy."

She forced a smile. She knew she shouldn't be angry with him. He wasn't responsible for that other woman's behavior. Yet she couldn't help how she felt. She watched him swing onto the back of the other horse and chided herself. All she should be thinking about right now was Katherine.

"What did the man say?" she asked.

"They turned left," he answered as they did the same. She could have told him that.

They followed the tracks out of town and up the slope toward Winter's Gate. The mud that slowed the buggy slowed them as well. Alfie tried to calculate how far ahead their quarry might be. At least in the buggy, Wingate wouldn't be able to turn off the road. They spurred the horses to as great a speed as was possible.

It was getting lighter now. To the west, across the valley, light was creeping down the peaks toward Glitter Creek. Here on this mountain, they were still in shadows. Alfie wished she hadn't looked back; she had to adjust to the relative darkness again.

In the road ahead a solid shape formed out of those shadows. "The buggy," Brian said.

She knew before they arrived that it was empty. She dismounted near it to look inside, hoping to find something that would offer a clue as to where its occupants had gone from there.

"Does this place seem familiar to you?" Brian asked.

Alfie turned to find him still in the saddle, studying their surroundings. "We've both been on this road before," she said.

"I mean this exact spot. Isn't this where we left the buggy when we came to see the ghost?"

Alfie couldn't be sure. But if it were, and Jason was headed for the same path, they would have to leave their horses behind. As she tied hers to the buggy she noticed an empty bracket where the buggy's headlamp should have been. A quick glance told her the other was still in place. She hurried around the buggy.

"A lantern will come in handy," she said when Brian joined her. She snapped the headlamp out of its bracket. "Jason took the other one."

"Their light will help us find them!"

"Ours could keep us from breaking our necks," she said, remembering her earlier trip on the rugged path in the dark. "Do you have any matches?"

"A few." He fished one out of a pants pocket and struck it, holding it while she raised the glass face on the lantern.

Alfie was worried. Even with the light, she wasn't positive this was the shortcut to the footpath they had followed before. They might be moving away from Katie instead of nearer. But it was the only direction away from the buggy that wasn't extremely steep. Even if they were right behind Jason, what exactly were they going to do when they caught up with him? She hoped Brian had a plan. She knew he had a gun.

But she would save that last worry for later. Moving quickly was dangerous on the uneven ground. The story Brian had told her of Jason's mother falling into a test hole came back to her. The slopes were covered with just such holes. Brian's hand on her arm was reassuring, but she knew that if she took one wrong step and began to fall, he would hardly be able to save her.

After only a few minutes, they came upon a narrow path and followed it. They moved even faster, but Alfie didn't trust the ground to be much safer.

A faint light flickered ahead. Alfie grabbed Brian's arm as she came to a stop, trying to catch sight of the light again. "Did you see that?"

"No. What did you see?"

"I thought I saw a light. It seems to have vanished."

Alfie remembered Katherine's description of the glowing ghost. What an odd thought. If she had seen a light at all, it was undoubtedly the other headlamp.

They moved on again, searching the trees ahead. "I must have imagined it," she decided after a few minutes.

"Which way?" he asked.

Alfie felt unreasonably warmed by his belief in her. "It seemed like it was a little up the slope from this path," she said.

"I'm afraid if we leave the path, we'll get lost. I'll look for signs of the direction that Jason might have taken. You watch for the light."

A few yards ahead, the path they were on took a hairpin turn. "They couldn't possibly have stayed on this path. Not if I truly saw their light," Alfie said.

"What else could you have seen?"

Alfie felt helpless. "I don't know. A reflection?"

"From what?"

He was right. The sun wasn't shining on anything on this side of the mountain. She tried to smile. "Maybe I saw the ghost."

Brian leaned toward her. "Do you realize how unfair that would be?"

She rested her head on his shoulder a moment, taking comfort in his presence. With a deep breath, she straightened. "I must have seen their lantern. If I did, they didn't stay on this path. We need to figure out where they went."

"And your best guess is . . ."

She closed her eyes, trying to remember exactly what she had seen, then pointed. "That way."

They had picked their way around rocks and trees for a few yards when their lantern light glinted off something on the ground ahead of them. Brian hurried toward it. "It's their headlamp," he said.

Alfie joined him and looked down at the broken lantern. It must have run out of kerosene and been tossed aside. Somehow it didn't seem quite right. Her thoughts must have shown on her face, for Brian asked, "What's wrong?"

"It seems like the light was farther away than this," she said.

"We've just come farther than it seems. But we're on the right track, Alfie. They can't be very far ahead of us. And they're moving in the dark."

"Jason might spot our light," Alfie said as they moved forward again.

"We're still better off with it lit," Brian said, urging her to move faster. The path was too steep for them to run; Alfie's skirts wouldn't allow it anyway. But Jason had Candy and Katie to contend with. Surely by now Candy realized the man meant her harm and would be resisting him. And Katherine? God, she hoped Katherine was all right.

Abruptly they left the trees and stepped out onto a cleared, though abandoned, road. Brian motioned for quiet and snuffed out the lamp. In the stillness they heard a woman's high-pitched complaint and a child's whine. Alfie felt hope surge in her breast, along with fear of what they would do once they actually caught up.

Brian took Alfie's arm and led her out onto the road, taking the upward slope. There were no trees here to filter out the predawn light, and in a moment their eyes adjusted. They could make out dark figures moving along ahead of them.

The road turned and followed the curve of the mountain's face. Alfie was so intent on the figures ahead that she didn't realize at once that the road ahead dropped into nothingness.

But she could still see Jason and the others moving ahead of them. They weren't walking on thin air.

A moment of standing with her toes on the edge of the broken road brought things into perspective. A landslide had carried more than half the road down the mountainside, leaving only a narrow ledge. That ledge was what Jason was traversing.

Alfie's heart sank. She turned to find that Brian had taken a couple of healthy steps away from the edge. His face was deathly white.

* * *

Brian hated himself for hesitating. It was light enough now to see the sheer drop-off quite clearly. He cursed, though he knew it was foolish to think the ledge would be easier to handle in the dark.

Alfie joined him and took the lantern, tying it next to her reticule at her waist. She took his hand and whispered something, something encouraging, he supposed, and urged him toward the ledge. He followed, trying to think of Katie and forget everything else.

He had barely stepped onto the ledge before his head started to spin. He quickly dropped Alfie's hand. If he fainted and went over the edge, he didn't want to take Alfie with him.

"It's all right, Brian," she said gently. "Just don't look down."

"It's hard to watch my step without looking down," he said, forcing a laugh.

She was ahead of him and he hated that. She shouldn't be between him and their foe. But they were already out on the ledge and there was no going around her, even if he could have brought himself to do it.

"I'm serious, Brian." She reached a hand toward him, and he took it, cursing his own cowardice, grateful for her strength. "Don't look down. Look at me."

He followed her, breaking immediately into a cold sweat. He wished to the depth of his soul that there was another way, but Katie was in danger, and now Alfie was, as well. He forced his legs to move.

With the morning light and the change in the terrain, they had lost their cover. Jason could notice them at any moment, if he hadn't already.

When the initial haze of fear had left him, Brian discovered that he could see Jason and his companions quite clearly over the top of Alfie's head. Jason was carrying Katie on one arm and pulling Candy along behind him. In spite of his fear, he and Alfie were making faster progress than Jason was.

He kept his eyes on his little girl and his mind on Alfie's hand gripped tightly in his. He moved his feet, determined that his fear wouldn't stop him from arriving in time.

Abruptly Jason and the others disappeared. Brian's heart lurched, and for an agonized second he thought they had fallen off the mountain. Then he recognized the dark hole of a mine tunnel in the side of the mountain, evidently what the road had been built for.

The knowledge was small relief. What might Jason be doing to Katie now? He had to know she was all right.

"Katie!" he yelled, startling Alfie.

"You might have warned me," she muttered as the echo died away.

"Daddy!" came the answer.

Jason stepped out of the mine, the child in his arms. Brian thought he heard the man laugh. If there had been any way to do it, he would have put Alfie behind him. The two people that mattered most to him were now both in danger, and he felt completely powerless. He wished to God he had left Alfie in town. Oddly enough, he hadn't even considered it earlier. And he wasn't sure he could have ventured out on this ledge without her. But back in town, at least she would be safe.

"Daddy!" Katie called again.

They were close enough now to hear Jason say, "That's right, call them in."

"It appears we're playing into his hands," Alfie said.

Brian didn't answer. The distance between them had narrowed until he could look his adversary in the eye. Anger was quickly replacing fear.

"Come on in and join the party," Jason said. "Try anything, and I'll toss the girl off this mountain."

Alfie released Brian's hand and went obediently into the mine. Brian paused in front of Jason. "Give her to me," he said.

"Give me your gun."

"I'm not carrying one," Brian said, opening his coat to show he wore no holster.

Jason shifted Katie and held her over the edge of the cliff. The girl terrified, stopped wriggling.

"Don't," Brian said, raising a placating hand. He eased the gun out of his pocket and placed it on the ground. "Give her to me," he said again.

Jason grinned and pointed inside.

Brian complied but stayed close, ready to spring toward Jason if he made the slightest movement toward the edge.

Once Brian was inside, Jason set Katie down and retrieved Brian's gun. The little girl ran into Brian's arms, and he held her tightly, feeling her heart racing against his own. She clung to him and he to her.

Brian knew that any chance of fighting Jason was gone as long as the child was in his arms. Though it took more strength than stepping out onto that ledge, he pried her arms from around his neck and whispered, "Go to Alfie."

Katie resisted at first. And Brian turned to find Alfie comforting Candy, who was lying on the floor, weeping. "Alfie," he whispered.

She looked up and he motioned for her to take Katie. She understood at once and came toward him. Brian saw her blanch and turned quickly.

Behind him, the legs of a man lay stuck out of the darkness. He turned Katie over to Alfie and motioned her toward Candy, farther away from Jason.

He didn't look toward the body again. "Thurston, I assume," he said to Jason.

"You're damn sharp, Reed. That's why you're going to die." As Jason talked, he took several sticks of dynamite tied in a bundle from his coat.

"That's a little foolish, don't you think?" Brian said, stepping toward Jason and trying to ignore the pistol leveled at his heart.

"No, I think it's brilliant. No one will ever find any of you."

"Some folks will think it's odd that we all disappeared, leaving rooms full of possessions."

"Oh, the possessions will be out of your rooms before noon. I'll get them." Jason attached a long fuse to one of the sticks.

Brian took another careful step toward him, but Jason reacted quickly, leveling the gun once more. He held it on Brian for a moment while they glared at each other; then Jason slowly turned the gun in the direction of the women and child. He kept his eyes on Brian's and laughed. "Ease on back," he said.

Brian stepped back, but only one step. "Marshal Hagman knows you left with both Candy and Katie."

"No kidding?" Jason asked, grinning. "So does the old coot at the livery stable. I took them to a doctor in Denver, and that's where they decided to stay. And you two got bored and decided to leave town. Nobody's going to care."

Brian remembered Thurston's empty room. "Why are you doing this?" he asked, moving farther away from the others, hoping to increase his chances of jumping Jason without endangering them.

"Because I worked all my life for that greedy old man for nothing! He's never forgiven me—never given me anything. I wanted the mine and I wanted to ruin him. And no two-bit whore and no out-of-town snoop are going to spoil that for me."

"You killed James and Perkins, then, didn't you? And Trebly?" Brian moved to the side a couple of steps, working himself a little closer to Jason. When Jason lit the fuse, the man would have to run to safety. Brian intended to be near enough to toss the dynamite out of the mine when he did.

"They had outlived their usefulness," Jason said. The way he was studying the walls of the mine made Brian nervous. "Except for Trebly," he added with a laugh. "He never was useful."

Jason evidently found what he was looking for. "Back off," he said suddenly, leveling the gun at Brian. "Back away or I'll shoot you now."

Brian moved away, torn between his desire to shield Alfie and Katie and his fear that they were in more danger if he was close to them.

The mouth of the mine was lit by the feeble light of early dawn. In that light, Brian could make out Alfie, standing silent but alert, holding Katie, whose face was buried in her neck. Candy was standing now, crying, but she was no longer hysterical.

Brian returned his attention to Jason and understood why he had wanted him farther away. He had found part of a packing crate among the broken timbers and debris, and he was standing on it while he wedged the dynamite in a crevice some ten feet off the floor. It would have been the perfect time to jump him, but Jason had forced him too far away, and there was no moving quickly over the debris that littered the floor. Brian wished he carried a second gun.

Jason worked quickly and jumped down from the box, which he promptly turned on its side and smashed. He shot Brian a triumphant grin.

"You're going to have trouble getting away on that ledge." Brian said.

Jason sneered. "Why, you think the explosion will knock me off? I appreciate your concern, but I'm not going back the way I came. I know every inch of these tunnels, and where they let out." He pulled a match from his pocket and lit the fuse. "Now, goodbye." He turned to make his escape.

Suddenly a figure flew past Brian, hurtling toward the startled villain. It was Candy.

"Get back," Brian yelled, running to Alfie. He hurried her and Katie deeper into the mine. Candy had thrown herself upon Jason and was scratching at his eyes. Brian heard Jason's yell and the report of a gun. Together, he, Alfie, and Katie fled deeper into the darkness. As he ran,

Brian turned for one last look at the monster who had caused so much pain in Glitter Creek.

Silhouetted against the opening of the cave, Jason struggled to break free of Candy. She clung to his legs even as her life bled out of her. Jason fired twice at her and then turned the gun at Brian. Bullets sparked against the cave walls. An explosion rocked the mountain.

Instinct made Brian turn and dive, trying to shield Alfie and Katie with his body. Dust and darkness enveloped him.

Chapter Fourteen

"Alfie!" Brian's shout broke through the rumbling echoes.

Alfie rolled off a bruised hip and adjusted the little girl, who was still in her arms. She tried to speak and coughed instead. "Are you hurt, sweetheart?" she asked after a moment.

Katherine whimpered, but Alfie felt her shake her head. "It's dark," she said in a choked whisper.

"We're fine, Brian," she called. "Are you all right?"

"Yes." She heard pebbles scuffing against the floor of the mine as he made his way toward her voice. "Do you still have that lantern?"

"Yes, but it may be broken." She fumbled for

it around the child in her lap. "I think it's all right," she said. "It landed on me rather than the other way around."

Brian found them, taking them both in his arms. "I'm sorry, Alfie," he whispered. "I should have stopped him."

"You saved our lives," she said.

Brian didn't answer. They both knew that being trapped in a mine wasn't exactly saved. But neither were they buried under a ton of rock. "What happened to Candy?"

"She tried to stop Jason. Maybe she wanted him to take her with him. She kept him from escaping."

Jason's death didn't improve their situation. "Got a match?" she asked.

In a moment a match flared, and Alfie held out the lantern. Brian lit it and set it on the floor nearby. Its soft glow chased away some of her fears along with the gloom.

"Are you sure you're all right?" Brian asked, taking Katherine into his arms.

"I've got a few bruises," Alfie said, flinching as she flexed her shoulders. She had twisted her body in an effort to avoid falling on Katherine, and she had taken the impact on her right shoulder and hip. She didn't think there were broken bones, but there was nothing to bc done if there were.

"You were very brave, Katie," Brian said.

"He wouldn't let me get my dolly," Katherine whimpered. "I was scared. Is he gone?"

"Yes, he's gone," Brian said.

"Aunt Candy's dead, isn't she?"

He cast a questioning look at Alfie, but she didn't have a clue how he should handle this. It hardly seemed important when chances were it was only a matter of time until they themselves were dead as well.

"I'm afraid so," Brian said gently.

A deep frown creased the child's forehead.

"Don't worry," Brian said, hugging her. "I'll take care of you." With forced cheerfulness he added, "Let's see if we can't find someplace a little more comfortable. At least someplace where we can lean against the wall."

He stood, Katherine in his arms, and reached a hand toward Alfie. She did her best to come to her feet without revealing how sore she was.

He put an arm around her as they moved toward the wall a short distance away. "You *are* hurt," he said.

She wasn't surprised that she hadn't been successful at keeping her pain from him. "Just bruised," she assured him.

He didn't look as if he believed her. He kicked some stones out of the way before setting Katherine down. Alfie sat down beside her, trying and failing to stifle a groan.

Brian took the lantern. "I'm going to check on the cave-in," he said. "Will you be all right in the dark for a little while?"

Katherine leaned close, wrapping both of her

little hands around Alfie's. "Now we're ready," the girl said.

Brian gave them a smile that was surprisingly reassuring under the circumstances. Alfie watched him walk away. She couldn't think of anyone she'd rather be trapped with. Of course, living with him held much more appeal.

She shouldn't give up, she told herself. Katherine needed her to be brave. They could find a way out yet. In a moment the only light was the faint glow that designated the corner around which Brian had gone. Hope seemed harder to come by.

Katherine shivered.

Alfie put an arm around her and pulled her closer. "Cold?" she asked.

"No," she said. "Just something made me shiver."

"Are you afraid of the dark?"

The little girl shook her head and most of her body. "I'm not scared."

The light grew brighter and Alfie whispered, "Here comes Daddy."

"I'm glad he's back," Katherine whispered.

"Me, too."

"What's all this whispering?" Brian set the lantern down at their feet and found a place beside Katherine.

"Girl talk," Alfie said, forcing a chuckle and winking at Katherine. "Can we dig our way out?"

Brian shook his head. "Not the three of us."

"Maybe Marshal Hagman believed your girlfriend—"

"Girlfriend?"

She ignored the interruption. "—and came after us. If they dig from the other side . . ."

"Yes," Brian said. "The explosion might have drawn someone's attention, too."

He said it, but Alfie was sure he didn't believe it. A crew would have a hard time working on that narrow ledge. But there was nothing to be gained by voicing their fears.

"She's not my girlfriend," Brian said after a moment.

"Who?" Alfie asked, feigning innocence.

"You called Honey my girlfriend." He looked as if this subject really mattered.

"Then why do you call her honey?" *Damn.* Deep down in her heart it did matter.

"Because that's how she introduced herself. It's her name. She's one of Molly's girls."

"I gathered *that*." Alfie kept her eyes on Katherine, whose head was bobbing sleepily. She brushed the little girl's hair away from her face. "Sleepy, sweetheart?"

Katherine nodded.

Brian bent over the child. "Did you hit your head, Katie?"

"No," Katherine murmured.

"Have you been up all night?" Alfie asked.

"I couldn't sleep during the day like Aunt Candy wanted," she said.

"You can take a little nap," Alfie said, lifting her to straddle her lap.

The child was adjusted comfortably and dozing before Brian spoke again. "Are you jealous?" he asked.

Alfie turned to look at him, keeping her face carefully neutral. "Of course not," she lied.

His response was a grin. It faded too quickly. "We should try to find another way out."

"What if there is no other way out?" Alfie hated to discourage him, but she saw no real chance of escape. Her hip hurt too much for her to want to walk around in what was probably a fruitless effort. "Let Katherine sleep a little while."

"Our light isn't going to last long," he reminded her. "I could take it and see what I find."

Alfie imagined being left alone in the dark and shuddered. "Why don't you put out the light now, if you want to save it?"

Brian didn't look pleased with the suggestion, but he went along. As he reached for the lantern, Alfie caught his arm. "You do have more matches, don't you?"

He grinned at her. "Four, to be exact."

In a moment they were plunged into complete darkness. Katherine didn't react, so Alfie assumed that she was already asleep. A couple of clicks broke the silence as Brian set the lantern aside. The complete lack of light was eerie.

"You doing all right?" he asked.

"Just dandy," she said. Somehow it seemed darker now than it had after the explosion. Perhaps because the dust and the echoes of the concussion had dominated her senses then. Now there was only darkness.

"We'll get out of here, Alfie," Brian said softly.

"I'm holding you to that," she said.

His arm went around her shoulder, and he slid very close beside her. "How can I make you more comfortable?" he asked. His lips were evidently about an inch from her ear.

"I wouldn't mind a kiss," she said, snuggling closer.

"I'll probably miss in the dark."

Alfie giggled and felt Katherine sigh. "Try closing your eyes," she whispered.

Brian's deep laugh stirred her heart. He kissed her cheek and she helped him find her lips. The kiss was more tender than passionate.

"I lied to you, Brian," she whispered.

"I forgive you," he said, kissing her again.

"Don't you even want to know what I lied about?"

He was silent for a moment. "Will I feel better or worse when I know the truth? Because if you're going to tell me your only interest in me is a story, I think I'd rather not know."

She smiled into the darkness. "No, it's the opposite. When I said I wouldn't fall in love with you, I wasn't being entirely honest. I was already in love with you." She leaned toward him, hoping for another kiss.

"Oh, I knew that," he said instead.

"How could you know that?" She hoped he could imagine her indignant glare.

"I told you. I could taste it in your kiss."

"That," she said slowly, "is the most ridiculous, romantic thing I've ever heard."

He laughed. "Actually, you're not a very good liar. You were saying you weren't in love with me while you were trying to coax me into bed."

"Coax!" It was hard to sound offended and keep her voice down at the same time.

"What? Are you saying I seduced you?"

She thought about that a moment, remembering her brazen invitation. "I believe I'm much more comfortable with that version of the story, yes."

He laughed again, a very pleasant, comforting sound. "Well, whatever, I'm glad you can admit that you love me. Is it safe to assume you want to spend the rest of your life with me?"

"Considering how long that's likely to be, I suppose I can make that promise."

"I'll hold you to it," he said, echoing her words of a few minutes before.

At that moment, Alfie realized how much she wanted a life with Brian. She even thought that she could become a good mother to Katherine; all she'd have to do was follow Brian's example. Now, she wished she had accepted his offbeat proposal without mentioning their imminent deaths. She felt tears form in her eyes and didn't try to fight them. No one could see them anyway. She hoped she died first, but she knew it would probably be the brave little girl. For a moment she wished they had all been killed by the cave-in. But then she wouldn't have had the chance to tell Brian that she loved him. . . .

He was quiet beside her. She was afraid her voice would alert him to her tears, so she let the silence merge with the darkness.

Alfie thought their situation was hopeless. Reason told Brian that she was probably right, but he couldn't make himself believe it. It wasn't that he believed they had escaped the explosion for some higher purpose. Logic told him they could still die slowly, sealed in the mine.

But if death was so close, it seemed to him, he wouldn't feel so damn good! And his future, outside the mine, was brighter than he had ever dared imagine it. Though it wasn't what he would have wished for poor Candy, with her dead and Alfie as his wife, adoption of Katie was practically assured. The two most precious people in the world would be his to love.

Dying instead just seemed too ludicrous.

So what were his choices? Dig out of the rubble, or find another way out.

The rubble had fallen in a pyramid shape, so the top would be the most narrow and most logical place to dig. Perhaps he had dismissed it a little too hastily. Of course, having Alfie admit that she loved him made him feel much stronger than he had when he had first assessed the situation.

Searching for another way out seemed a shot in the dark. He grimaced at his own metaphor. They might walk within a few feet of an exit and not even realize it. The chances of losing their light before they found a way out were way too high. Their headlamp had already burned longer than he'd expected to need it.

As soon as Katherine woke up, he would move them closer to the entrance and go to work on a hole near the top of the rubble. If the light went out, he would keep on working. For Alfie and Katie, surely he would have the strength.

"Alfie?" he queried softly.

"Hmm," she mumbled.

"I have one more question; then I'll let you sleep."

"I'm not going to sleep," she whispered fiercely. "It's too damn dark to sleep."

Brian laughed, thinking how good it felt and how foolish it was to take delight in her indignation. "What does LV stand for?"

She laughed softly. "What difference does it make?"

"Well, it just seems like I ought to know before you sign some strange name on our marriage license."

She was quiet for what seemed like two full

minutes. "All right. I'd swear you to secrecy but that seems a little overdone, considering the circumstances."

"I'll never tell a soul."

"Leigh Vie."

Brian was sure he hadn't heard her right. "Your father named you Levi?"

"Two words," she corrected. "Leigh. Vie. He named me after himself, though. He thought he was extremely clever. He called me Leigh for a few years, then gave up and called me LV like everybody else. I think I'd rather you stick with Alfie."

He smiled to himself. He really liked the sound of that. He had every intention of sticking with Alfie.

He let his charges rest, listening all the while for any sounds of activity outside the caved-in entrance. When he could contain his restlessness no longer, he spoke softly into the darkness. "Would you mind if I left you for a few minutes?"

An arm shot out and caught him in the chest, and fingers tightened around his shirt. "You're not going anywhere without us."

He took the hand and brought it to his lips. "I'm sorry, but I want to get started digging."

"So we're back to digging now? What happened to exploring the mine?"

"I think you were right. I think we'd get lost and run out of kerosene and be worse off than we are now."

"If you're going to dig, we're going to help you." She slipped her hand away and shifted.

"Don't try to get up. Let me light the lantern and take Katie."

He leaned forward, feeling carefully for the lantern. Just as his hand contacted with it, something soft brushed across his face. In an instant it was gone, leaving him wondering what he had felt. Hair, he thought. Katie had sat up, and he had brushed against her hair.

He struck the match, lit the lantern, and turned to find Katie and Alfie as he had last seen them, Alfie leaning against the wall and the child asleep on her lap. What had touched his face? A bat? He hadn't heard anything. Perhaps he had imagined it.

He lifted Katie off Alfie's lap. She settled against his shoulder without waking. He reached a hand down to Alfie, helping her to her feet. She tried to hide the pain she felt when she moved, but he could see it in her eyes, even in the poor light. "You are hurt, aren't you?" he asked softly.

"I feel like I was thrown off a horse." She forced a smile.

He wished there were something he could do to help her. Finding a way out, he decided, he would help the most. "Can you get the lantern?" he asked.

"Sure." She bent slowly to pick it up, favoring her right side.

And something brushed against Brian's face!

There was no bat; he would have seen it. It wasn't Katie's hair; he'd had his hand on top of her head when it brushed him. He held still, waiting for it to come again.

Alfie watched him curiously. He would have liked to explain, but he had no explanation.

"There it is again," he said aloud. This time he thought he recognized it. "A breeze?"

"What?"

"I think I felt a cool breeze on my face." He pointed ahead of him, deeper into the mine. "If there's a breeze, there's another way out."

She turned, facing the same direction. "I don't feel anything."

"I don't either. Not now."

Just as he said it Alfie gasped, bringing a hand to her cheek. "What was that?"

"A breeze?" he suggested, hoping she'd agree.

"It felt odd."

"Maybe that's because of the atmosphere in here. Alfie, I think our best bet is to follow it."

She shifted the lantern to her other hand and slipped her free hand into his. He wondered if her ready agreement had more to do with resigned complacency rather than with any faith in this particular course of action.

Brian started down the tunnel, a sleeping Katie on his shoulder and Alfie at his side, wondering if he was leading them toward salvation or away from it. Just when he was considering turning back, the breeze came again, directly in his face. "Did you feel that?"

"No."

But she trusted him enough to follow.

Katie stirred, lifting her head. She rubbed her eyes and put her head down again. "Where are we going?"

"We're exploring," he said brightly. He hated to promise that he was taking her out of the mine when it might be quite the opposite.

The intermittent breeze led them deep into the mountain, or so it seemed; then the tunnel ahead of them branched off in two directions. Brian raised his hand, testing first one way, then the other. "Do you feel anything?" he asked Alfie, who was doing much the same.

She shook her head.

"What's she supposed to feel?" Katie asked.

Brian smiled at her. "A breeze," he said. "We're following a breeze."

She squirmed to be put down, and Brian set her carefully on her feet. He crouched down in front of her. "Are you sure you weren't hurt when you fell?" he asked, not wanting to let go of her until he knew she was fine.

"I'm not hurt," she said, leaning forward to kiss his cheek. "I missed you, Daddy."

"I missed you, too." He touched his finger to her nose and she shivered, making them both laugh.

"It's gone." Alfie had spoken very softly, hoping, he supposed, to keep from sounding as desperate as she looked.

Brian stood, wondering if he should try

using a match to locate the breeze, and someone blew in his ear. Or at least that was what it felt like.

"This way," he said, leading them to the right.

The floor of the mine sloped upward, giving them the illusion, at least, that they were getting nearer to the surface.

"How did the breeze go around a corner?" Alfie asked.

"I'm not an expert on wind currents," he replied.

"And as long as you don't know that it's impossible, you aren't going to worry about it?"

"Hey, I believe in ghosts. What can you expect?"

This made Katie giggle. The giggle, probably more than the remark, made Alfie turn and smile at him.

Her smile faded with the light. They were in darkness again.

He heard the rattle as Alfie shook the lantern. There wasn't the faintest sound of liquid. "Now what?" she asked.

He heard Katie whimper. "Take my hand, Katie." He reached toward the sound. She was moving toward him, too. She bumped his leg, and he lifted her into his arms.

"Keep a lookout for even the faintest light," he said.

"I see a light," said Katie.

"Where, sweetheart?" Alfie asked.

"Right there." She was evidently pointing.

Brian didn't detect the faintest glimmer of light in any direction. He was about to ask her to show him with his hand in hers when the breeze hit him right in the face. He heard Alfie gasp a moment later.

"You felt it, too," he said. "We're getting closer."

With Alfie pressed against his side, he moved his charges ahead very slowly.

"There must be some bushes or something covering the hole, so only gusts of wind make it through," Alfie suggested.

That was as good an explanation as any. His current fear, besides the obvious ones of walking into a rock wall or falling into a pit, was that the hole would turn out to be a hundred feet above their heads.

Brian tried to calculate how far they had moved in the dark. Beyond the reach of the lantern before it had gone out? Farther? They still seemed to be working their way uphill.

He felt Alfie tense beside him. "Stop," she said. She tried to pull away from him, but he wouldn't let her go.

"Let's not get separated," he said.

"There's a wall right here," she said, moving away until their arms were both outstretched. "I don't know if the tunnel turns or branches or just plain stops."

"We should go that way," Katie said.

Brian had no idea which way "that" was. "Did you feel the breeze?"

"I can see the light. We should go this way." She turned his head with her hands on his jaw. "Don't you see it?"

And something, maybe Katie, blew in his face. But it didn't smell like Katie. It smelled old, somehow. Musty.

"She thinks we should go right again," Brian said.

"Breezes are bad enough, Brian. I'm not going to believe she sees lights around corners."

"Do you have a better idea?"

"Yeah. Let's use up a match making sure there is a right."

He wouldn't let go of her until she was near him again; then he found the match in his pocket, carefully transferring it to Alfie's hand. Alfie lit it and held it up to reveal a tunnel leading off to their right. She looked back, took his hand, and smiled, just as the flame flickered out.

"This way." She pulled him toward his right.

He caught up and slowed her down. "Think bottomless pits, Alfie," he whispered. "Think jagged rock walls."

"The light's right there," Katie said.

And Brian saw it. Far ahead and what looked like only a few feet off the ground was a crescent of light. Odd that this close he could no longer feel the breeze. And somehow the light didn't seem like sunlight.

As they made their way toward the light, Brian heard the hollow clank of iron on rock.

The sound, though faint, grew louder with each step. "Glover's mine," he said.

"What?"

"Glover's mine. He said his tunnels were getting so close to Wingate's that one day they'd bump into each other. I thought he was exaggerating."

Brian carefully passed Katie off to Alfie, then hurried ahead of them, shouting as he went. After a moment he fell silent, listening. The clanking he had heard earlier had stopped. He gave one more shout and waited.

Alfie came up beside him, feeling her way in the dark. "Is someone there?"

"Yes," he whispered. "Listen."

Brian could hear voices now, too muffled to understand but definitely voices. He realized they could see the hole between the tunnels because of the lantern light on the other side. The miners had no such advantage. He might have succeeded in getting their attention, but now he had to let them know where they were.

With his arm around Alfie again, he moved closer to the hole. It was too high for him to reach. "If I lifted you, could you reach into the hole and get their attention?"

"I could try," Alfie said.

Katie had to be left standing alone out of harm's way, but she didn't seem frightened now. Perhaps the light coming through the small crescent was enough to reassure her that they would soon be rescued. It reassured Brian.

Lifting Alfie until she could reach the opening wasn't as easily done as he had expected. The total darkness that surrounded the opening had made it seem closer than it really was. Before Alfie had succeeded in reaching it, a tiny cascade of pebbles and dust trickled out and a voice echoed through the tunnel, "Is somebody there?"

All three yelled their responses at once. Even Katie got in a good shout for help.

"How'd you get in there?"

"Never mind," Brian called. "Just get us out."

"Stand back," the miner shouted. "We'll make the hole bigger."

Brian returned to Katie and drew her and Alfie farther from the hole. As the rocks fell away he said softly to Alfie, "I kept my promise."

"What promise was that?" she asked.

"To get us out of the mine."

"You got us out?"

He smiled and shrugged. "What about your promise?"

The light coming though the opening was bright enough now that he could make out Alfie's location, but not her expression. When she didn't answer, he clarified. "You said you'd live with me the rest of your life."

He hadn't known how she would react, but laughing hadn't been his first guess.

"You're holding me to that?"

"Absolutely."

He was still waiting for Alfie's response when a miner's head and torso poked through the hole, blocking most of the light. "You still there?"

"Of course we're still here." Brian hadn't meant to sound so irritable. He wasn't as happy to be rescued as he ought to be. He had hoped to get this settled with Alfie first.

"Hand me a lantern," the miner called behind him. In a few minutes pale light filled the tunnel. "That's quite a drop," he said.

He disappeared for a moment; then a rope snaked out of the hole and dangled almost to the floor. "You first, Alfie," Brian said.

The miner returned, holding the lantern for light while Brian helped Alfie tie the rope around her waist. The light disappeared again as the miners pulled Alfie up.

"You're next, Katie," Brian said when Alfie was safely through the opening. He turned to find Katie's attention elsewhere. She was waving her little fingers at nothing.

"Whatcha doing, sweetheart?" he asked, moving to crouch beside her.

Katie turned and smiled shyly. "Just saying 'bye to the ghost we were following."

It took nearly an hour for Glover's miners to get all three of them through the opening and then to the surface to safety. They brushed the dust off each other, and Brian took a deep breath of fresh air, thinking how incredibly beautiful

Alfie looked with her face smudged and her hair in disarray.

One of the miners ran to get his boss, and Brian wanted to resume the discussion he had been having with Alfie before they had been interrupted. Alfie, however, was deep in a conversation with Katie. The child was telling her about the ghost.

Glover joined them in a matter of minutes and listened while they told him about Jason's kidnapping and their escape from the explosion. He took them down the mountain in his own buggy and left them in front of the hotel, promising to tell their story to the marshal.

"I wonder if Hagman will come to talk to us," Alfie said as they walked up the steps behind Katie.

"It's hard to tell with Hagman. He might simply take Glover's word for everything and figure the case is closed—but it's not. Kline was Jason's partner. Together, they essentially stole the mine from Jason's father. Our testimony can help Dale Wingate reclaim it. If Hagman won't listen—"

Brian stopped her at the top of the stairs and turned her toward him. "That's not what I want to talk about; we can handle that later. We didn't finish our conversation."

"What conversation was that?" she asked, smiling.

Brian resisted the urge to sigh. "The one about promises. I wanted to tell you that I can promise you plenty of travel, and you could write articles while you're at it. I'll move my business to Denver, if that's what you want."

She blinked. "Are you offering me a job?"

This time he did sigh and watched her grin. "I'm asking you to marry me. I can't be a daddy without a mommy beside me."

"Well, in that case," Alfie said with a smile, "of course."

She stepped into his arms. He kissed her, conscious of Katie watching them. He didn't end the kiss until he heard the little girl giggle.

SURRENDER to the FURY

CONNIE MASON

Five years after Nick Drummond swindled her father out of everything he owned and left Aimee LaMotte with an illegitimate child, he reenters her life a Union soldier as the South lies in flames. And though the beautiful belle's heart cries out for revenge, she is undone by the unexpected gentleness and nobility of the man who wronged her years before. She cannot deny the irresistible desire that draws her into the powerful, loving arms of her enemy, and forces her to surrender to the fury.

___52266-7 $5.50 US/$6.50 CAN

Dorchester Publishing Co., Inc.
P.O. Box 6640
Wayne, PA 19087-8640

Please add $1.75 for shipping and handling for the first book and $.50 for each book thereafter. NY, NYC, and PA residents, please add appropriate sales tax. No cash, stamps, or C.O.D.s. All orders shipped within 6 weeks via postal service book rate.
Canadian orders require $2.00 extra postage and must be paid in U.S. dollars through a U.S. banking facility.

Name____________________
Address____________________
City____________________ State______ Zip__________
I have enclosed $__________ in payment for the checked book(s).
Payment must accompany all orders. ❑ Please send a free catalog.
CHECK OUT OUR WEBSITE! www.dorchesterpub.com

The West–it has been Loralee's dream for as long as she could remember, and Indians are the most fascinating part of the wildly beautiful frontier she imagines. But when Loralee arrives at Fort Apache as the new schoolmarm, she has some hard realities to learn...and a harsh taskmaster to teach her. Shad Zuniga is fiercely proud, aloof, a renegade Apache who wants no part of the white man's world, not even its women. Yet Loralee is driven to seek him out, compelled to join him in a forbidden union, forced to become an outcast for one slim chance at love forevermore.

___4267-3 $5.99 US/$6.99 CAN

Dorchester Publishing Co., Inc.
P.O. Box 6640
Wayne, PA 19087-8640

Please add $1.75 for shipping and handling for the first book and $.50 for each book thereafter. NY, NYC, and PA residents, please add appropriate sales tax. No cash, stamps, or C.O.D.s. All orders shipped within 6 weeks via postal service book rate.
Canadian orders require $2.00 extra postage and must be paid in U.S. dollars through a U.S. banking facility.

Name____
Address______________________________________
City____________________State______Zip__________
I have enclosed $__________ in payment for the checked book(s).
Payment must accompany all orders. ❑ Please send a free catalog.

Heartland

Rebecca Brandewyne

After her best friend India dies, leaving eight beautiful children in the care of their drunken wastrel of a father, prim Rachel Wilder knows she has to take the children in. But when notorious Slade Maverick rides onto her small farm, announcing that he is the children's guardian, Rachel is furious. Yet there is something about Slade that makes her tremble at the very thought of his handsome face and sparkling midnight-blue eyes. And when he takes her in his arms in the hayloft and his searing kiss brands her soul, Rachel knows then that the gunfighter Slade Maverick belongs to her, body and soul, just as she belongs to him.

___52327-2 $5.50 US/$6.50 CAN

Dorchester Publishing Co., Inc.
P.O. Box 6640
Wayne, PA 19087-8640

Please add $1.75 for shipping and handling for the first book and $.50 for each book thereafter. NY, NYC, and PA residents, please add appropriate sales tax. No cash, stamps, or C.O.D.s. All orders shipped within 6 weeks via postal service book rate.
Canadian orders require $2.00 extra postage and must be paid in U.S. dollars through a U.S. banking facility.

Name____
Address____
City______________________State________Zip__________
I have enclosed $__________ in payment for the checked book(s).
Payment must accompany all orders. ❑ Please send a free catalog.
CHECK OUT OUR WEBSITE! www.dorchesterpub.com